Jesus My Son

Mary's Journal of Jesus' Early Life

Mary Bailey

authorHOUSE®

AuthorHouse™
1663 Liberty Drive
Bloomington, IN 47403
www.authorhouse.com
Phone: 1-800-839-8640

First published by AuthorHouse 2/25/2010

ISBN: 978-1-4490-6495-2 (e)
ISBN: 978-1-4490-6493-8 (sc)
ISBN: 978-1-4490-6494-5 (hc)

Library of Congress Control Number: 2009913897

Printed in the United States of America
Bloomington, Indiana

This book is printed on acid-free paper.

For nothing is impossible with God.
Luke 1:37

Preface

Did Mary really write a journal? Most scholars will say girls during Mary's time were not able to write. But is it possible? Yes, it is and how much better is Jesus' story when written by His mother. There is so much during Jesus' early life that only Mary would know. If we are not allowed to believe she wrote these events for us to know the true Jesus, how will we ever learn of them?

During a sermon one Sunday morning, God lit a spark in my heart. I realized Mary was a mother with feelings and emotions, not just an instrument to fulfill God's plan. Once the fire was lit, it couldn't be extinguished. In fact, the flame was continually fueled from other ministers and events. Whenever I reached an obstacle I couldn't resolve, God provided a practical solution in most unusual ways. From Mary's view, Jesus' early life comes alive in this journal. Get to know the young Jesus as I have through many hours of research, in-depth Bible study, real life experiences and an imagination that God allowed to run a little wild at times.

Acknowledgements

I would like to thank the following ministers
for their role in inspiring this book:

Joe Brown who initially ignited the spark

John Gillum, Scott Johnson and James Driver who fueled the fire

Tod Schwingel

whose thought provoking sermons nurtured my desire to
dig deeper in the scriptures in search of the truth.

Thanks to Anna, Mary, Betty, Todd, Diana, and Debbie
for their edits, prayers and encouragement

Jimmy Johnson for the illustrations

And to those many websites from which I gleaned
information regarding customs during Jesus' lifetime.

Special thanks to

Virginia Smith and Next Step Critiques!
for in-depth editing and recommendations
that made my story much richer.

And last, but not least, I thank God for allowing me
to believe this really might have happened.

This book is dedicated to:

Darrel

Todd and Mary Elizabeth
Joey and Julie

and my grandchildren:

Chase
Sydney
Zachary
Sheridan
Suzette
Saylor

and especially Autum
who taught me to Google for my research.

My journal is as full of love as Mary's.

Table of Contents

In the sixth month, God sent the angel Gabriel to Nazareth, a town in Galilee, to a virgin pledged to be married to a man named Joseph, a descendent of David. The virgin's name was Mary.
Luke 1:26-38

Mary's Inspiration to Begin this Journal

Greetings! My name is Mary and I have become the most blessed woman in the whole world. The angel Gabriel visited me and has completely altered my life. His visit has inspired me to begin a journal to record this amazing journey. How else will the world know about the events of God's son as seen through the eyes of his mother? God's son—yes, that is what the angel said. I have no idea what I will be writing in the days to come; but if the angel's words are true and I do give birth to God's son, many great things will happen because of this child.

Why did God choose me? I have struggled with this question. Are there no more worthy virgin girls for this special event that has been proclaimed by many of the prophets? Most of the girls my age are devoted to serving our Lord. I am no more virtuous than any of them. Although I try to keep my mind clean and pure, I struggle with the same thoughts as all girls my age have. There are many who are prettier, wealthier and even poorer than I am. Some have beautiful voices that sound like the nightingales when they sing. My voice may sound more like a screechy owl, but I still love to memorize and sing the Psalms of King David. I am a simple peasant girl with no unique qualities.

The only difference between me and the other girls is my ability to read and write. Fortunately, my parents believed in the importance of education for girls as well as boys. Whenever lessons were being taught in our home to my older brother, Judas, they insisted that my sister, Salome, and I also participate. Since both my parents work closely with the priests in the synagogue, they have access to the parchment and papyrus that is left from the priest's studies. They bring home every scrap piece of writing material and every extra drop of ink they can find to encourage us to write as much as we can. I love to see a written page full of beautiful words. Expressing my feelings through poetry is my favorite pastime. Like the patriarch, David, with his holy verses of praise, my love for writing is only second to my love of serving my dear Lord. It now appears I will be able to do both of my favorite things for the rest of my life. Perhaps God knew I would be compelled to record the events of his son to tell the world things that only a mother would know. That surely is one of the reasons God chose me.

When the angel appeared to me, I was so frightened I could not breathe. At thirteen, I have studied many of the scriptures and know about angels communicating with people and about God talking to people in dreams. Sarah bore a child after she was beyond childbearing years. Hannah was told of Samuel's pending birth. Oh, there are many other visions and stories of the Lord selecting someone to do His will. Never in my wildest dreams did I think I would ever join this circle of great people. I feel blessed, but also frightened.

Early this morning I knelt by the window for my daily devotion while waiting for the sunrays to warm the chilly morning air. Suddenly a bright light burst through the window. In the midst of the light the angel appeared, and said, "Greetings, favored one! The Lord is with you." I was troubled at his saying and wondered what manner of salutation this could be. The conversation has bounced around in my mind many times until it is etched there forever. The angel continued, "Do not be afraid, Mary, for you have found favor with God. And behold you will conceive in your womb and bring forth a son, and you shall name Him Jesus. He will be great and will be called the Son of the Most High; and the Lord God will give Him the throne of His father David; and He will reign over the house of Jacob forever, and His kingdom will have no end."

My body froze as my mind raced. Kingdom, son of Most High— what did the words mean? Throne of David? Is my son to inherit all of David's riches? Is this truly the Messiah we have been waiting for who will recapture and restore the throne of David? My racing mind slowed enough for me to ask how this could happen since I am still a virgin.

The angel told me that the Holy Spirit will come upon me, and the power of the Most High will overshadow me. For that reason, the holy child shall be called the Son of God. Overshadow me? What does that mean? How will this come to pass and…will it hurt? He said that my cousin Elizabeth had also conceived a son in her old age, and she who was called barren is now in her sixth month. I'm sure the angel meant to ease my fears and anxiety when he added, "For nothing will be impossible with God."

All I could say was, "Behold, the bond slave of the Lord; may it be done to me according to your word." The angel left and I could only stare in amazement. I pinched myself to make sure I wasn't dreaming. My body seemed to be frozen for hours.

What can this possibly mean to me? Remembering the scriptures I have read and heard, I know that someone is coming who will build a mighty kingdom. But will my child be this great king? How can that be possible? I am nothing—a simple peasant girl. My stomach is full of butterflies with questions. What will my dear Joseph think? I must deal with that tomorrow. This great honor brings enough worries for one day. A kingdom? My dear Lord!

Surely others will record the great events of the son of God. My son. But none will see him as I do. The views I have will be much different than those of others. For one thing, there are not many women scribes and I don't think any other person will be focusing on the events of Jesus' life as I will. Since women are not held with the same respect as men, many will think my view is not important. This story has to be an exception. Surely God chose me not only because of my devotion to him, but also because of my love for writing. He knew I would preserve these events for all generations to know the truth. I must use all my skills to record my story faithfully.

Dear God, I stand in awe at this blessing You have bestowed upon me. Thank You for the wonderful opportunity to serve You and write beautiful stories for the rest of my life. Now that I have reasoned why I may have been chosen, I beg you to help me make the most of this ability and create something that will help the entire world better understand some of the most intimate things concerning Your son. Things that at times, I must store in my heart until I am able to scribe them. Please give me the ability to recall all things as accurately as You would have the world know them. May the stories be as beautiful and blessed as I trust the journey will be. With pen in hand, I am prepared to be the vessel that will pour out the truth as only a mother can—deeply, from my heart.

"The Holy Spirit will come upon you, and the power
of the Most High will overshadow you.
So the holy one to be born will be called the Son of God."
Luke 1:31 & 35; Matthew 1:18

Mary Conceives a Son

Today my pen is ready to write, but my mind is empty. According to the angel, last night I conceived a baby who is truly God's son. How did You do it? When Your Spirit overshadowed me, I felt Your presence, but there was no physical interaction. My body was floating on a sea of radiant light as the power of the Most High overshadowed me and I received the seed of Your Holy Spirit. I awoke this morning knowing that my body had conceived the beginning of the baby of the angel Gabriel's announcement. My Lord, You chose me for the ultimate blessing among women, but I am beginning to have second thoughts about this blessed journey.

We have long anticipated the Messiah, but I certainly didn't think He would come from me. Why would God choose me? He knows I am young, shy, and engaged to… Oh, my dear Joseph! My sweet handsome Joseph with his thick brown curls hanging to his shoulders. His big strong hands will stroke his thin scraggly beard as he contemplates the news. Those dark brown eyes will search deep into my soul. What will he think? How can I tell him? What will he say? He is such a kind, considerate man, but this will be hard for even him to believe.

Should I tell him God forced me? Would that make it better for him? But what would that do for my baby who is really God's child? God did not force me. Why was I so willing when the angel appeared to me? I should have asked more questions, but my mind was racing so fast I didn't have time to think of anything. "Behold the bond slave of the Lord; may it be done to me according to your word," is what I said.

Wait! Why am I worried? I am carrying the son of God. Joseph and my parents will be as delighted as I am, won't they? I am glad Salome and Judas have married and moved away from Nazareth. I can see Salome's doubting look if I had to tell her. Judas would raise his eyebrows in disbelief. I can't say I blame them. I would be very doubtful if they told me such unbelievable news.

Right after I came into womanhood at age thirteen, Joseph, following the customs of our people, told his parents of his wishes to purchase me as his bride. His parents talked to my parents. Soon our entire neighborhood knew of the negotiations taking place. Joseph's intentions became the center of conversation as the women met at the well. Even Joseph's boss teased him. At eighteen, he is an apprentice carpenter and is assumed to be a serious-minded young Jew. He is regarded as a responsible adult capable of supporting a family.

Of course, I wasn't supposed to know these talks were taking place, but rumors spread like a raging fire in a town like Nazareth. My parents were also aware of my desire for Joseph as a husband. Soon Father and Joseph agreed upon a price. My father has chosen not to tell me how much I am worth. Joseph and I drank from a cup of wine over which my father pronounced a betrothal benediction and the marriage covenant was established. We were formally betrothed and were considered married by Jewish law. In some areas of Judea this covenant would even allow sexual relationships to take place, but in Galilee purity is maintained through the final marriage vows. We are now in the period of separation which could last up to twelve months.

Everyone knows that it takes a man and a woman to conceive a child, but beyond that I have little knowledge. The day I became a woman I couldn't even tell my mother. I wanted to hide until it all went away. I survived that, and surely I will survive this also. From what I understand, I won't be having any kind of monthly woman's times for about nine months. I *think* this will be a typical pregnancy. Since God is in charge, He can do anything He wants.

My dear God, how can I do this? Why me? I love You with all my heart, but I am still afraid. Never in my wildest dreams, did I expect to be blessed like this. Though I am having mixed feelings about calling it blessed.

What are my parents going to say? They know Joseph and I are fond of each other. Mother and I have had our little "talk" and I have dreamed of becoming Joseph's wife on our wedding night. Joseph is kind and considerate, but I can also sense the passion he holds for me. He is older and more knowledgeable than I am about worldly things that happen when people marry. In my dreams, he slowly shows me all those things

I've heard from the women at the well. I can't wait for these dreams to become a reality.

My ink is running low, but I have much more to write. I have no other way to express myself or keep all this fresh in my mind. Journal, you must become my secret friend to whom I can bare my soul.

Dear God, if You trusted me enough to give me this blessed child, please give me the right words to explain to Joseph and my parents. Even better, please let the angel appear to them like he did to me. I don't want to have to tell them. Give me the strength and wisdom I need to get through this trying time.

Because Joseph was a righteous man and did not want to expose her
to public disgrace, he had in mind to divorce her quietly.
Matthew 1:19; Luke 1:36-37

Mary Tells Joseph she is with Child

I rushed to Joseph's shop early this morning with the exciting news. Since we are supposed to avoid contact during this period of separation, he quickly pulled me inside and scanned the area to make sure no one had seen me.

"Mary, what are you doing here?" he asked as he grabbed my shoulders and searched my face for some sign of what could have caused this excitement.

The words poured from my mouth until I saw his face writhe in pain.

"How can this be? Are you not a virgin?" he asked as his big strong hands stroked his thin scraggly beard and… he turned away.

I ran from his shop before the deluge of tears burst from my eyes. The tears are still pouring as I write this. My heart is heavy because of the hurt I caused him. The unbelievable news caused him much distress. Joseph has always known of my complete innocence. He is understandably shocked beyond measure that I am with child. Does he believe I have been unfaithful to him? Why didn't the angel appear to Joseph and tell him also? Why would God allow this heartbreak when the truth is bright and beautiful? Joseph feels betrayed by the innocent girl he deeply loves.

By Jewish law, Joseph has some options. He could divorce me publicly and be compelled to tell the elders why. Then if I was found to be with child, Joseph would have to swear that he had no carnal knowledge of me and I would be judged to be an adulteress. The only penalty for that is stoning. The townsmen would lead me to a cliff and make me jump or push me. Then they would throw rocks at me until I no longer moved and I would be left for the animals and birds to finish. I know in my heart that my dear Joseph loves me too much to allow that, no matter how disappointed he is in me.

He could also choose to have me put away privately where I could have the baby in secret and remain there. His only other option is to swallow his pride, proceed with the wedding and let people wonder about the short pregnancy.

Should I drink some of the bitter herbs I have heard the girls at the well talk about that would end this pregnancy and possibly my life? Oh, that horrible thought hurts my heart. Forgive me, Lord, for even thinking of destroying your son.

I feel Joseph has in mind to send me away quietly to spare the disgrace. I am positive he no longer wants me for his wife. He turned away and all my dreams were destroyed. And for what? If God chose me, why wouldn't He help make it easier for those around me? I will never forget that look of pain on Joseph's face. That look of total amazement followed by total disbelief told me he will never trust me again.

I must leave here to avoid that same look of disappointment from Mother and Father. They will be supportive because they love me. But they will be disgraced among their friends and family. People will talk about me behind their backs. I don't think I can stand to see them face that shame. Where can a young girl with child safely travel? I should be afraid, but when I think of the events that brought me to this point, my fears disappear. If God trusted me enough to carry His son, I am confident He will show me where to go and will take care of me wherever that path may lead.

I will write Mother and Father a letter and pack a few things and…I know! I will go visit my cousin Elizabeth. Yes, that is it. God *did* show me the way. Why else would the angel have mentioned Elizabeth's pregnancy? God knew of Joseph's reaction and gave me a sign to tell me where to go. Elizabeth can help because she is also with child. I must recognize and believe these signs and trust that God will continue to show me the way. Elizabeth will understand and not condemn me. Even though she is older, she has always been one of my favorite cousins. She can help direct me because she also truly loves my God. Now I think I can quit worrying and move forward. For the first time in two days, I am at peace with what is happening to me. My fear and anxiety are gone.

Dear God, I pray that You will continue to show me the direction You would have me to go and give me wisdom to make the decisions I know I must make. I pray that You will send an angel to help my mother and father and my dear Joseph understand what has happened.

Mary Writes a Letter to her Mother and Father

Dear Mother and Father,

This letter will be a shock to you, but I believe you trust me enough to know that there is a reason for what I am doing. I must leave for a while. Please don't follow me. There is something I must do. I am going to visit Cousin Elizabeth. Remember the travelers the other day who spoke of an old priest struck deaf by an angel? His wife was with child even though she is well past her time of child bearing years. You thought that sounded like Zechariah and Elizabeth. Since you had not heard anything, you dismissed it.

*Well, they **were** talking about Elizabeth and Zechariah. I know because an angel told me she is about six months pregnant. Yes, an angel visited me! It was a remarkable experience, but it may cause you some sorrow and embarrassment. I have decided to go help Elizabeth for a while to give me time to clear my mind and think about all that has happened.*

I hope you will receive a heavenly visit to explain everything. Don't worry about me because I will be safe. In fact, the Lord has blessed me beyond any of your expectations or mine. This is hard to understand, but for now please trust me. God has truly blessed me and will keep me under his care. I am sorry for any pain or sorrow this will cause you among your friends, but you must believe that I have done nothing wrong in the eyes of our Lord.

You may want to talk to Joseph, but don't be surprised if he doesn't want to talk to you. Although he knows my story, he has not received the understanding from God to accept it. I pray that he and you receive a visit to explain what is happening. When God tells me it is time, I will return, but for now please love me as you always have. I need the strength that comes from your love.

Love with a special part of my heart,
Mary

P.S. Dear Father, I am sorry we will not finish the game of senet we began last night. I want to thank you for teaching me the games that in the eyes of most people are reserved for the men of our village. I thoroughly enjoy playing senet with you. You have been a wonderful teacher and father. I promise we will finish that game someday.

Mary Writes a Letter to Joseph

My Darling Joseph,

I am sorry to do this, but I must. My heart is crushed by the pain and sorrow I have caused you. Please know that I have done nothing wrong. I hopefully you will receive an explanation for all of this soon and that look of disappointment on your face will be replaced with one of understanding. I truly do love you and was looking forward to becoming your wife. Now I am afraid that may not happen because I don't think you want me anymore. If I were you, I would feel the same way. Please know that I love you too much to be unfaithful to you. There is no other man I desire. The disbelief and disgust in your eyes told me that your love could never be the same.

I am going away while you consider your options. It is a big decision, but I truly believe that you will find some guidance along the way. When you do receive an answer, please do not feel badly. I fear you will feel such anguish when you learn the truth, but please know that God has a reason for everything. When this is over, I pray our love will be deeper than any of the oceans God created.

My dear Joseph, my only prayer is that our loving God will help you understand the circumstances surrounding the child I carry. Although I don't understand, I still believe God has plans for me. I will follow the obscure path He has placed under my feet until He gives me a clear view of the road ahead.

I hope to see you again soon. Until we meet again, please know that I will always love you with a special part of my heart.

Mary

Mary's Journey to Visit Elizabeth

We have stopped for the night which gives me a chance to write about my traveling experience. The last few days have been tiring, but I have met some nice people that I know God sent to me. The young couple I am traveling with now has promised to take me all the way to the temple where Zechariah is a priest. If he is not there, surely someone can tell me where he lives.

Intense fear gripped my entire being as I set out from Nazareth alone, carrying a few clothes in a bundle, and this precious journal. I only knew that Zechariah was a priest and he and Elizabeth lived in the hill country of Judea, but I was determined to find them. I have been to their house with Mother and Father, but I don't remember how to get there.

I had walked a very short distance, when a huge caravan with camels, loaded with spices and food and all kinds of goods, came along the trail. The kind caravan master invited me to travel with them as far as Sychar in Samaria where they were stopping to disperse their goods. Although my parents refused to travel through Samaria, I felt comfortable traveling with the caravan. That night, lying safely by the bright fire on a blanket the master had given me, I thanked God for watching over me and asked for His protection as I continued my journey through Samaria.

The caravan arrived at its destination the next day. The caravan master wished me well and told me the location of Jacob's well, where I would most likely find people who might be traveling farther. Dusk began to blanket the area as I retrieved a refreshing drink from the well. Fear of starting out on that strange road alone joined with the deep loneliness that often comes with the night.

As if reading my mind, a young Samaritan woman who came to draw water, asked if I needed help. I was unsure how to perceive the foreigner, and nervously explained that I had been traveling with the caravan that arrived today. Since darkness had already set in, I was reluctant to start out again. Sensing my fear, she asked if I would care to spend the night with her and her aunt. I was uncertain about staying in a Samaritan home, but my desire for safety overruled my doubts.

The young girl, Christina, lived in a rundown house with an aunt who suffered from every known ailment. I had the impression she did not welcome a Jewish woman to enter her home. From what I could see, the aunt's ailments were more in her head than in her body. Although I was the one being helped, I felt pity for the young girl who had to endure the constant orders of her demanding aunt.

After a restless night, I woke up early the next morning to a delightful smell coming from the clay oven. Christina had prepared some sweet cakes and had packed a few supplies for my journey. She never asked what circumstances had compelled me to be traveling alone, but I sensed she knew of a sad story behind my journey. I hugged and thanked Christina as I slipped quietly away before her aunt awoke from an herb induced sleep. As I waved good-bye, Christina looked as if she longed to escape with me.

I had not traveled more than a few minutes when another caravan heading toward Jerusalem invited me to travel with them. Thankful for such good luck, I started to accept their invitation when I noticed Christina far back on the path running toward us waving her arms aimlessly. I graciously declined their invitation, which resulted in more than a few curses from the master, and ran back to meet Christina.

"I am glad I caught you," she said as she struggled to catch her breath. "I saw that caravan leaving right after you left and I knew I had to warn you. That is not a good caravan master. He has the reputation of being the most crooked dealer of them all. I had to catch you before they "invited" you to join them. His men are all know to frequent the prostitutes when they come to Sychar. Please come back home with me. I know a wonderful neighbor family who is making the trip to Jerusalem tomorrow. You can ride with them until you reach your destination."

Grateful for a safe ride to Elizabeth's, I readily accepted the invitation and thanked God for again watching over me. There wasn't any urgency in my trip, and spending the day with Christina might help me forget my loneliness for Joseph and my parents. I helped Christina complete her chores, and then we walked through the village of Sychar shopping, but mostly looking, at the various shops. The gruff man at the sandal shop eyed Christina lustfully as she hurriedly pushed me past his door. Tears filled my eyes when we passed by the carpentry shop. As Christina stole a glance at the handsome young man crafting a beautiful cedar box, my heart yearned to be home in the comfort of Joseph's presence.

We spent the rest of the day talking and laughing with Alexa, the woman who agreed to take me on the rest of my trip. When we were leaving, her husband, Silas, arrived home. He jokingly asked Christina if she could join us on our trip. Obviously, Alexa and Silas were not happy with the situation of Christina and her aunt.

Christina told me a little of her story as we walked back to her house. When she lost her mother, her father had requested that her aunt come and help care for her. Shortly after that her father died, leaving her at the mercy of the always sickly, demanding aunt. I felt pity for the new friend God had shown me. How heartbreaking to be forced to sell the house her father had worked so hard to build. But there was hope that the young shepherd boy of the village would soon visit her aunt to purchase her for his wife. She smiled as we entered the door barely hanging from its worn leather hinges.

The aunt, anxious for Christina to return, immediately began barking demands. Christina shrugged and performed her nightly pampering routine for her aunt without a complaint. Thankful for the reprieve from my own problems, peaceful sleep came quickly that night and stayed till the morning dawn. Bright and early, Alexa and Silas arrived to pick me up on their way to Jerusalem. Christina and I hugged and vowed that our paths would meet again someday.

As my journey will end tomorrow when we reach the temple, I am nervous about the greeting I will receive from someone as righteous as Zechariah and Elizabeth. Will they be as doubtful as Joseph when I told him my story? They may even consider me unclean since I am traveling with these wonderful Samaritans and spent the night in a Samaritan home. I pray my Lord will give me the words to help them understand.

Thank you, dear Lord, for carefully watching over me and for these new friends You have graciously given me. All my life I have thought of the Samaritans as someone with whom we should not associate. Now I see them as one of Your own creations. I know our meeting was more than a coincidence. I will long remember the young Samaritan woman at the well.

where she entered Zechariah's home and greeted Elizabeth.
Luke 1:5-25; 39-58

Mary Visits Elizabeth

This morning as we neared Jerusalem, Silas asked a man leading a donkey with a cart full of goods if he knew where the priest, Zechariah, lived.

"You mean that priest whose old wife is having a baby?" the man asked scornfully.

When Silas indicated that was the one, the man pointed to the hills and said they lived south of Jerusalem. Silas thanked him and we continued on our way.

The man uttered as he led his donkey down the road, "Don't understand why anyone their age would want a baby."

We traveled a little farther until Silas and Alexa reached the turn for their destination. I hugged and thanked the dear new friends for allowing me to travel with them. They promised to watch after Christina when they returned to Sychar.

The lump in my throat grew with every step I took along the path to the hill country. A woman in the first house of the village pointed to a small house set back against the hill when I asked if she knew where the priest, Zechariah, lived. As I approached their door, I noticed some cracks in the clay walls and a few holes in the clay covering the branches on their roof. It was evident they were no longer able to make necessary repairs.

My apprehension turned to delight when I arrived at Cousin Elizabeth's house. I knocked and watched as she slowly drug her slumping body with her bulging stomach to the door. I could not believe what happened the moment she saw me. Her face lit up as her worried frown turned into a glorious smile. She knew! Her baby leaped in her womb and she was filled with the Holy Spirit. She cried out in a loud voice, "Blessed are you among women, and blessed is the fruit of your womb. And how has it happened to me that the mother of my Lord would come to me? When the sound of your greeting reached my ears, the baby leaped in my womb for joy. And blessed is she who believed that there would be a fulfillment of what had been spoken to her by the Lord."

When she finished speaking, a song came into my heart. I couldn't stop singing. The angel must have given me the beautiful words. For a moment my voice sounded like a nightingale. The words poured from my soul, and they still resonate within me. They're forever burned in my heart.

> *My soul exalts the Lord,*
> *And my spirit has rejoiced in God my Savior.*
> *For he has had regard for the humble state of his bondslave,*
> *For behold, from this time on all generations will count me blessed.*
> *For the mighty one has done great things for me;*
> *And holy is his name.*
> *And his mercy is upon generation after generation*
> *Toward those who fear him.*
> *He has done mighty deeds with his arm;*
> *He had scattered those who were proud in the thoughts of their heart.*
> *He has brought down rulers from their thrones,*
> *And has exalted those who were humble.*
> *He has filled the hungry with good things;*
> *And sent away the rich empty-handed.*
> *He has given help to Israel his servant,*
> *In remembrance of his mercy,*
> *As he spoke to our fathers,*
> *To Abraham and his descendants forever.*

I told Zechariah and Elizabeth about my trip and was relieved when they seemed pleased that God had provided a shelter for my safety even though it was in a Samaritan home. God certainly directed me to Elizabeth's house. I am content to stay until He wants me to leave. She needs my help through her pregnancy and I know I can learn much from her. Being pregnant at her age, I expected her to look bad. How wrong I was. How can anyone who is beaming as she is, look bad? Poor Zechariah, he cannot speak as a result of the angel's visit. I expect the news was quite a shock. As old as they are, they are truly going to have a baby. Elizabeth stays inside all of the time to avoid the reproachful looks from some of the women who think she is foolish for even trying to have a baby at her age. Although she is proud to be carrying this child, she is content to stay inside.

Joseph, Mother and Father seem far, far away. I pray that God has eased the pain and sorrow for them. Although I know my abrupt departure was a shock to them, I had to leave. As soon as God tells me, I will return home, but for now Elizabeth and I have much to share. We are like lost sisters who have found each other. Our age difference means nothing when we share such a wonderful bond.

Dear God, thank You for leading me to Elizabeth to watch and learn from her years of wisdom. Help me recognize and believe the signs You send to help me along this journey. You have truly blessed me among women.

Elizabeth Receives a Cradle

Since my arrival over two months ago, Elizabeth and I have shared such wonderful times. Each day brings a new blessing and sometimes a new heartache. She has been such a comfort to me when I think about Joseph and home. I am amazed at her story and am compelled to record it also. When Zechariah came home after the angel's visit, he wrote everything he could remember. Sounds like my visit with Gabriel. The words hung in my mind, I could recall every one. Although Elizabeth is not able to read, she learned most of the story from what the other priests were telling and from Zechariah's hand movements and facial expressions. She was delighted, and also surprised, that I was able to read Zechariah's entire account of the incident. Apparently, he has chosen not to show his writings to anyone else.

Zechariah had been chosen by lot, according to the custom of the priesthood, to burn incense on the golden Alter of Incense in the Most Holy Place. This solemn ceremony is considered a great honor since a priest can only perform it once during his lifetime. If the lot had not fallen upon Zechariah that day, he would surely not be alive when the rotation of the twenty-four groups again came to his division.

Zechariah was in the temple burning incense while a group of assembled worshipers were praying outside. Gabriel, the same angel who appeared to me, did indeed enter the Holy Place and speak to him. Zechariah must have been as awestruck as I was. According to his account, the angel's words were, "Do not be afraid, Zechariah; your prayer has been heard. Your wife Elizabeth will bear you a son, and you are to give him the name John. He will be a joy and delight to you, and many will rejoice because of his birth, for he will be great in the sight of the Lord, he is never to take wine or other fermented drink, and he will be filled with the Holy Spirit even from birth. Many of the people of Israel will he bring back to the Lord their God. And he will go on before the Lord, in the spirit and power of Elijah, to turn the hearts of the fathers to their children and the disobedient to the wisdom of the righteous—to make ready a people prepared for the Lord."

Zechariah questioned the angel's words because he is an old man and Elizabeth has long passed the childbearing years. It surprises me that Zechariah, as righteous and devout as he is, would dare question the angel's words. I don't feel bad about my reaction now. Evidently Gabriel wasn't too happy about Zechariah's doubts either, because the angel told Zechariah he would be unable to speak until the day this proclamation is fulfilled.

Elizabeth and Zechariah know of the prophecies of a Messiah and the one who will prepare the way for him. They are convinced our sons will fulfill these two prophecies. Elizabeth knows with certainty that we are a big part of God's plan. She is so happy and I am so afraid.

I have shared my journal with Zechariah. He smiled when he read about my reaction to Gabriel's visit. When he read about the Holy Spirit overshadowing me, he raised his praying hands to the heavens as tears poured down his cheeks. His head turned back and forth in disbelief as he read of Joseph's reaction. We hugged and the deluge again erupted from my eyes. It still hurts to think that Joseph did not believe me. My heart aches for him to know the truth.

With Elizabeth bedridden, I am learning how to complete her chores. My mother often allowed us to study while she did the housework. I am not nearly as skilled in duties of the house and cooking as most girls my age. This is a good experience to prepare me for the wife I hope to be some day. Elizabeth will not let any of the other women help her. They don't understand why she is having this baby at such an old age. Since I do understand, we are enjoying this time and I am learning much that I need to know about carrying my baby.

God could take away all the pain and discomfort that accompanies carrying a child, but evidently my time is going to be like all others. My symptoms of morning sickness, nausea, and increase in appetite have been the same ones Elizabeth had. I know God sent me here to realize that. No matter what happens, I truly know that God is in control.

The strangest thing happened today. My mother and father sent a beautifully crafted cradle for Elizabeth's baby. I recognized Joseph's handiwork in the excellent craftsmanship. He is such a wonderful carpenter. In my dreams, I still watch him craft his furniture. It has always amazed me that he could take some rough pieces of wood and create such beautiful masterpieces.

The messenger who delivered the crib today also brought a note from Mother and Father. It said they hoped I would return home soon. They want to share in my happiness. They were in the process of making a cradle for my child also. Tears poured from my eyes. Evidently they have discussed my situation with Joseph. I know they are telling me "All is well. Please come back home."

It tears me apart to think that I have put my parents through all this turmoil. They are considerate, selfless people who were always good about teaching me. They love me and will forgive me, but because of my hasty and unexplained departure, I fear I have shamed them in the eyes of their friends.

I trust that God will show me when to go home. He knows I am needed here and that I must learn all I can from Elizabeth and Zechariah. But I miss everyone—especially Joseph. If he is still working, he must have not been too hurt by my leaving. I wonder if he thinks of me as much as I do him. Is he working on a cradle for my baby, which should have been our baby? I am anxious to get home now. Elizabeth is close to her due date and I know God will direct me to go home when she no longer needs my assistance. After the birth, she will be willing to let the other women help.

The mornings are beginning to be a little rough. Elizabeth said she had morning sickness for a month and could eat nothing but bread and water. She said Zechariah's compassion and care saw her through that trying time. I know Joseph would be the same way if he believed my story. Elizabeth passes me an understanding glance when I push the food away and quickly take off running or rush outside as soon as I get up in the morning.

Dear God, please give me the strength to get through this trying time even if I have to do it alone. I understand now a lot of things concerning this birth. It all has to be normal, doesn't it? I must strive to give this child an ordinary life until You are ready to take over. Please give me an understanding heart when that time comes.

When it was time for Elizabeth to have her baby, she gave birth to a son.
Luke 1:56-66

John the Baptist is Born

I am sorry I haven't written like I should have, but Elizabeth and I have been busy. John arrived eight days ago and I am going home tomorrow. This birth has helped me learn much about my own impending birth. God surely directed me here to provide insight into what I must do when my son is born. We have spent three lovely months together growing with God and with child.

Giving birth placed a strain on Elizabeth's worn and aged body, but God has truly blessed her with this son. Everything went as God told them it would. When they came to circumcise the baby, Elizabeth told everyone his name would be John, but the men of their family completely ignored her. As soon as Zechariah wrote "John" on the slate, the Holy Spirit filled him and he spoke. He began prophesying and blessing God as I did that day I entered their house.

Everyone agreed that he should be called John. The men in the family were surprised at his name because there is no one else named John in their family. What will people say when I name my baby Jesus? We don't have any one named Jesus in our family, either.

I could see people asking "Who is this young girl and when did she arrive here?"

Since Elizabeth and I stayed close to their house these three months, I had not met many women of the village. Elizabeth had not welcomed anyone into her house while she was with child. At least, no one noticed that I had gained a little weight while I was here. With the many layers of loose-fitting garments we wear, I could carry this child for a full term and no one would ever know. All I would have to do is gather the outer tunic in the front and loosen the belt as needed.

I am glad I could stay and help Elizabeth the last three months she was carrying John. With his birth last week, I am preparing to go back home. Elizabeth assured me that God had taken care of everything and all would be well. When I lay John in the beautiful cradle, I know she is right. Elizabeth's years of knowledge and her wisdom are gifts from God.

She asks for wisdom daily and it is apparent that God grants her request. Her wisdom is far above most of those men at her house today.

Tomorrow one of her neighbor families is allowing me to travel all the way to Nazareth with them. The trip home proves to be much different than the one here for I know this particular family will skirt around Samaria. I will miss stopping at Sychar to visit Christina, but perhaps that will happen another time. I am getting anxious to return home and see what God has prepared for me.

Now that John is born, Elizabeth will have all the help she needs from other women in this town. As the angel commanded, Zechariah will ensure that John will be a Nazarite from birth. They both obey God completely without question. I still sometimes have questions. My youth and inexperience is completely opposite of Elizabeth's deserved status. My status doesn't matter, I know that I am having God's son, and that I have not known any man.

God, how did You do it? I can feel the presence of Your tiny baby as it grows in my belly. The experience most girls have when they become with child is still unknown to me. When people ask me how this child came to be, what can I tell them? I beg You to give me the wisdom to face my parents and Joseph and all those friends and family who are going to question my earlier escape from home.

Why would anyone think that I would be the chosen one? I know I would not think that about anyone I know. There is no woman in the world worthy to do what You have called me to do. I am afraid and also blessed. The song I sang when I first saw Elizabeth poured from my heart to thank You. Why I, among all women, would be chosen to carry this precious baby that is going to save the world is beyond my comprehension. That thought carries a lot of reason for concern. If I find it hard to believe, how will my baby ever convince people that he truly is the Messiah we have been expecting?

What will be my role in this kingdom that You have chosen for my son? This baby is Yours completely, but he is also mine. He will take nourishment from my body for nine months. He will drink from my breasts for two years. How can I bear to give him back to You? How long will You allow me to hold him and nurture him as I have seen Elizabeth do John?

I hope Elizabeth and I can talk and compare notes after my baby is born. Even though we may be far apart, we will be together in spirit. Even now her presence is with me as I prepare to go home. In a few days my desperate escape will come to an end and I will have to face those from whom I ran. Before I change my mind and decide to stay here with Elizabeth, I must put away this pen and get some things together for my trip. First, I must write Elizabeth and Zechariah a letter to thank them for all they have done.

Dear God, I pray for the insight and acceptance that is such a part of Elizabeth's life. Help me make it a natural part of mine as I return home to continue this blessed journey You have mapped out for me and my baby. Thank You for the time You have always allowed me to write when an event needs to be preserved.

Mary Writes a Letter to Zechariah and Elizabeth

Dear Elizabeth and Zechariah,

Thank you for allowing me to spend these last few months with you. Although my trip here was a desperate escape, I know that God sent me to your house for a reason. The minute I walked in your door and the angel sent me the song, I knew I had followed God's direction.

Watching you grow with John and helping with his birth was the best thing that could have happened. At least I now know what to expect during this pregnancy and have some idea of what is going to happen when I give birth. Spending time with you has been the most rewarding experience I could have received.

God is present in your home and everything you do. Your love for Him has nurtured mine. He has come alive for me since I have been here. The future is still uncertain for me, but I do know that I will be blessed because you will be praying for me daily as I will for you and your son.

John is such a beautiful little baby. I hope he and his cousin, Jesus, will become good friends. We must visit as often as possible. Your devotion for our Lord has been such an inspiration to me. Thank you again for your hospitality and all that you have taught me and for drying my tears the many times I missed my family and Joseph. My heart is deeply yearning to go home now because you have proven to me that all is well.

Thank you and please know that I will always love you with a special part of my heart.

Mary

Mary stayed with Elizabeth for about three months and then returned home.
Luke 1:56
"The Lord does not look at the things man looks at…"
I Samuel 16:7

Mary's Trip Home

The family that offered me a ride to Nazareth had a cart for us to ride which made the trip home much faster. That was the first time I had traveled in a cart. The cart made the trip faster, but did not make a smooth ride. I would have preferred walking. When we reached the fork in the road that led to Sychar, I wanted to stop and visit my friend Christina. I knew that would be impossible when the man pointed his finger down that road and said, "You be very careful, young lady, and *never* travel through that land. Those people are unclean."

This man and woman are righteous and devout people. Why would they think someone as kind as Christina would be unclean because of her beliefs or where she lives? I saw Mount Gerizim where Christina worships. To the Samaritans their mountain is the true sanctuary chosen by Israel's God. Are they wrong because they chose to worship on a mountain instead of in a temple? I still hope to see my friend, Christina, again someday.

When the family reached their destination a short distance from Nazareth, they offered to take me the rest of the way to my home. I declined because I wanted to spend some time alone. My first instinct was to run home as quickly as possible, but I still had some anxiety over the greeting I would receive. The message sent with the cradle told me all was well at home. Does that mean they have received divine insight explaining this child I am carrying or does it mean they think I have sinned and they forgive me? I felt a need to stop and write about my feelings. I am sick, but I don't know if it is from the butterflies in my stomach or from the child that is throwing my body into all kinds of fits. This child, God's son, is quickly growing. There, I said it again. It is true and I know I must make everyone else believe me, especially Mother and Father and Joseph, my darling Joseph. I hope he has not forgotten me in the three months I have been visiting Elizabeth.

When I left, Joseph thought I had been unfaithful to him. The wonderful life we could have together may not happen. My love for him has not died these last three months. In fact, I love him more now than ever. He is the soul mate God made for me. The next step is totally in God's hand. Joseph looked forward to showing me all he could and helping me learn the ways of a woman. Now he thinks I have learned from someone else.

I am not sure if the angel has appeared to Joseph and told him the circumstances surrounding this baby I am carrying, I only know that God will show me the way and I must accept whatever happens. I will always love Joseph with all my heart. When I see his face, I will know if he has been enlightened by the truth or if he still doubts my story.

He may be angry because I left, but I had to give him some time. If he chooses to have me put away privately, I will accept that as a part of God's plan. Surely he loves me too much to have me stoned as an adulteress. He would not be able to live with himself with that choice.

I can only imagine the ridicule Joseph has endured since I have been gone for such a long time. I didn't know what else to do. When I realized the angel had not appeared to Joseph and told him about my baby, my heart shattered. With Elizabeth's insight, I now realize God chose not to tell Joseph for a reason. It is unbelievable that this divine conception could happen to me or anyone I know.

Suddenly I feel unworthy to complete this assignment, and yet God saw something worthy in me. After Zechariah regained his speech, he read about Samuel anointing David. I heard him say, "The Lord does not look at the things man looks at. Man looks at the outward appearance, but the Lord looks at the heart." Yes, I must always remember that God looked at the heart of many women, but He chose me. I will shout it from the mountaintop if I must—I am going to be Jesus' mother!

Dear Lord, please give Joseph the understanding to know that I still love him with all my heart and give him the ability to understand everything about this baby I am carrying. I also pray Mother and Father have received an explanation. As my desperate escape comes to an end, the fear and anxiety I am feeling are overshadowed by the determination I have to be the best mother You ever created.

An angel of the Lord appeared to him in a dream, saying,
Joseph, son of David, do not be afraid to take
Mary home as your wife, because what is conceived in her is from the Holy Spirit."
Matthew 1:20-25

Mary is Welcomed Home

I finally found enough nerve to travel the short distance remaining to reach Nazareth. My heart felt like it would explode from my chest when I saw Mother and Father standing in the doorway with outstretched arms. My tears were moving as fast as my feet by the time I reached them. What a relief to know that they know the whole story. The angel *did* appear to Joseph and told him not to be afraid to take me as his wife. Joseph knows the child I am carrying is truly conceived by the Holy Spirit. He will not have to question my faithfulness anymore.

My parents said they were heartbroken when they first read my letter. Father, thinking the worst, rushed to Joseph for some answers. He found Joseph curled up in the corner of his shop sobbing uncontrollably.

"What have I done?" he asked Father. "I didn't believe her and I forced her to run away. She had no choice. A moment ago the angel Gabriel also visited me and told me not to be afraid to take Mary as my wife because what is conceived in her is from the Holy Spirit. The angel said Mary will give birth to a son and we are to name him Jesus. Why didn't the angel appear sooner? If I had only known"

Joseph hung his shoulders and told Father it may be too late for me to forgive him. Father listened as Joseph related the meeting with me that morning. Joseph was devastated that he had not believed me.

"How could I have been so blind?' he asked Father. "I knew Mary would not be unfaithful. She is the most righteous young woman I know. I must find her and tell her how sorry I am. Do you know where she might be?"

Father was relieved to know that something miraculous had happened instead of something tragic. He handed Joseph his letter, but did not mention the other one I had written to Mother and him. Father, in all his wisdom, thought it best if Joseph did not know where I had gone. Since the angel did not appear to Joseph until after I left, Father thought God had a reason for sending me away. Father was willing to let God complete His plan. I also think Father may have been angry with Joseph for doubting my story and wanted him to think about it for awhile. Father later asked Joseph to make the cradle for Elizabeth, but never mentioned the message Mother sent. Joseph never knew I had gone to visit Elizabeth. That was a relief, because I often thought that if Joseph really loved me, he would have come to take me home. Father knew that we needed that time apart and that if we were meant to be together, God would find a way.

After reassuring Mother and Father that I still loved Joseph and knew that he was the soul mate God had chosen for me, they sent for him to come to the house. He ran through the door, grabbed me around the waist, picked me up and swung me around. His reaction surprised me, since he is not one to show a lot of emotion, especially in front of my parents. Thankfully, the closed door kept the neighbors from seeing his actions. When he arrived, Mother and Father wisely walked outside. He hugged and tenderly kissed me and told me how sorry he felt for the way he acted. He said he had initially intended to divorce me quietly without saying anything, but the angel appeared to him and told him everything that had happened. Shame haunted him for not believing me. He couldn't wait for my return. The look of happiness on his face now has completely erased that look of disappointment he wore when I left three months ago.

Why did I doubt God? Why didn't I believe that He would take care of everything? I knew He could do no less than He always has—love His children. And truly it had to be this way. Otherwise I would never have gone to see Elizabeth. Those were the best three months for me. My relationship with God has grown much with the nurturing of Elizabeth and Zechariah. They gave me the strength I need to get through this pregnancy. The experience of watching John's birth taught me more than anyone could have told me about childbirth. I know that experience will help in about six months. Who knows? I may be in some desolate place without anyone to help.

At this point, I can't see that happening since Joseph bought us a house while he waited for me. He said he knew I would return and he wanted to be ready to perform the marriage ceremony as soon as possible. He showed me the house this afternoon. It is small and set back against a hill. It has two rooms. The first is for Joseph's shop that already contains all the tools needed for his carpentry business. The back room has an earthen oven that is about three feet deep, six feet wide and two feet high. I will cook all our food there. I can't wait to fix Joseph our first meal. Thank goodness, I did learn something about cooking while visiting Elizabeth.

The top of the oven will be our bed. On our wedding night Mother and Salome, if she is here, will place candles and lace around to prepare it for our "marriage bed." The heat from the oven will warm our bodies, but I also expect to be warmed from the heat of Joseph's body. There is a short table next to the oven. Maybe some day we will eat sitting on chairs like the wealthy. Perhaps when Jesus has his kingdom, we will have chairs and tables to entertain the royal visitors. Our lives will most likely change considerably when our little king receives his kingdom and crown. What kind of a mansion will it be? I'm sure he will welcome me and Joseph to live with him. He will not be like some of the kings who forget their family as soon as they receive that power. Next to the table is a wooden tether for our donkey who will be my companion as Joseph works in his shop. I will practice singing my lullabies to him.

God always has a reason for doing what He does and everything that has happened since my meeting with the angel is proof of that. Joseph had time to think about what he needs to do. He wants to forego the rest of the period of separation and perform the marriage ceremony as soon as possible. I am relieved that I will not have to bear this baby alone in shame. He has also promised that we will not consummate our marriage until after the birth, so the child will be born of a virgin, as the prophets have foretold. He also may be afraid of harming this precious baby.

God must also know that Joseph is a righteous man. My heart is telling me that after this tumultuous beginning we will have a wonderful life together. It will be interesting raising this baby that we know we must give back to God someday. That may be a lot harder than it seems right now. As confusing as it all is, I am thankful that I will not have to do this alone. God has surrounded me with wonderful, caring people… who are eagerly awaiting instructions for this wedding. I must begin some quick planning.

Thank You God for a Father whose wisdom compares with the great Solomon. His patience allowed the love Joseph and I share to reach full maturity. You have given me a most gracious blessing. Tonight I am more blessed than the wealthiest person in the world. No earthly riches can come close to comparing to the love of a family and my soul mate that I know You have chosen for me.

Mary Prepares for her Wedding

It is official. Tomorrow Joseph and I will be married. Our union will be blessed by a few of our friends and family. Mother and I jumped for joy yesterday when Salome and Daniel arrived with their son, John. They moved to Capernaum a month after their baby was born to take care of Daniel's sick relative. We had not seen them for seven months. Mother had sent a message of our wedding, but wasn't sure it would reach them in time. It didn't, but Daniel needed to come to Nazareth to check on something with his kinsmen. At the last minute, they decided to bring their son to see his grandparents and aunt. God does work his wonders at the most favorable times. Maybe Judas and his family will show up also.

Many of our guests may be suspicious of the conditions leading up to this hasty event, but Joseph and I do not care. God is the only one we have to please. Many wedding ceremonies last for a week. Ours will only be one day. We haven't had a lot of time for preparing a big event. We didn't want to invite anyone except family and a few close friends who would not question the circumstances surrounding our wedding. Everyone in the town knows that I have been gone a few months and when I show up with a bulging stomach in four or five months, they are going to question my faithfulness to Joseph. It doesn't matter. We both know that this wedding is another small part of God's wonderful plan.

Joseph told me he is worried that he will not know what part he is to play in Jesus' life or how he can best interpret the will of God. He is also worried about the prophecy of the Messiah that is supposed to be born in Bethlehem, the city of David which is at least a five days journey from Nazareth. We have no intention of moving or going there for anything. We will have to wait to see what God plans for us.

All the preparations have been made. Mother has cooked enough food for an army of hungry soldiers. We plan to have the ceremony outside where a priest will preside over all the details. Mother has made a beautiful veil and dress that will cover any signs of the baby I am carrying. Not that I am ashamed of it. In fact, I am so proud of this baby, I want to shout it to the world that I am carrying our Savior. Only I don't think many would believe me. I am only a lowly peasant girl from Nazareth and everyone knows that nothing spectacular ever happens in Nazareth. How hard will it be for my son to convince everyone when he must begin his mission? People are not going to believe him either. I wish I could pave the way for him, but Cousin John will have to do that since God chose him also. I hope he and Elizabeth are doing well. I think about them often and wish I could go back and see them soon.

Dear God, please bless our union tomorrow. You have already shown that You approve or You would not have appeared to Joseph. He is still as much in awe of what happened as I am. Thank You again for the wonderful blessing. Help me to be worthy of raising this child, as You would have me do. I am still Your servant and will do whatever You ask of me. Although I want desperately to tell this good news to everyone I see, give me patience to wait for Your appointed time.

And Joseph did as the angel of the Lord commanded him, and took Mary as his wife,
Matthew 1:24-25

Joseph and Mary are Married

Today is my wedding day and I am sitting on the floor writing in my journal tonight. This is not how I had dreamed of spending this night. I thought I might experience the stories the girls told when they gathered at the well after their wedding nights. My story will be lacking some of the adventure, but they will all know that Joseph is a wonderful husband.

My wedding was beautiful. I'm grateful my parents were willing to work hard through the past week. Mother prepared an enormous feast which pleased everyone. The gorgeous weather allowed us to take advantage of the omen that with an outside wedding we will be blessed with as many children as stars in the heavens. The heavens were exploding with stars tonight. We already have a start on our children.

Mother found some satin and draped it over four poles for a canopy for us to have a simple traditional ceremony. Our attendants were Salome and Joseph's brother, Alpheus. I circled Joseph seven times, which is the tradition to show him how central he is to my life. We received the seven blessings, which join us as a couple to our community. I accepted the ring from Joseph.

After we drank our glass of wine, Joseph stepped on the glass and broke it. This tradition enables us to reflect on the destruction of the temple in Jerusalem. This act probably meant more to us than it does most people. I couldn't help but think that someday this baby may live in that temple.

I was sorry Judas and his family did not attend, but I am sure they didn't receive the message in time. Everyone thoroughly enjoyed the fellowship as they consumed the feast Mother and her sisters had prepared, and drank freely from the abundant wine supply. Wine is usually the most important element of any celebration. To run out of wine at a wedding ceremony is a disgrace. I'm happy to report that we had plenty.

When people first arrived, there were a few whispers among the women about my three-month absence. Mother convincingly explained that I had gone to help our cousin Elizabeth during her pregnancy since her age prevented her from doing any housework. Most believed her and were understanding. I don't think anyone suspects that I am now three months with child. I know no one suspects how I conceived this child.

After the ceremony, Joseph took me to our new house. He gently carried me through the doorway and tenderly laid me on our marriage bed. Then he lay down beside me. His arms engulfed me in an enormous compassionate hug that left no doubt in my mind that he completely believes my story. He truly is mine. With help from the wine, he quickly drifted off to a peaceful slumber. Unable to sleep, I slipped from his arms and our marriage bed to write while everything is still fresh in my mind.

As I look around at our small, simple room with the meager furnishings, I can't help but wonder about the throne of David the angel told me would be my son's. How soon will all this take place? Until it does, I am content to share this humble home with the man I love, and our donkey, and our son when he is born.

The blessings I have received are many, but I would have loved to truly become Joseph's wife tonight in every sense of the word. As Joseph promised, we will not have any relations until after this child is born. I can tell he loves me deeply, but as it should be, he loves his God more. He does not want to do anything to His child. I agree. I have been chosen and, as I told the angel, I am the Lord's servant to do as He directs me.

Watching Joseph sleep soundly in the bed above the stone oven, I long to be there with him. There is a yearning in my body that I have never experienced before. I want to fully love and cherish him. He is my life now, and I will strive to be the best wife ever.

Joseph told me his heart shattered when he learned that I had left. When the angel appeared to him and told him the truth, he felt such guilt. My father had given him my letter, but didn't tell him where I had gone. He was so devastated, he had to talk to someone. He told his brother, Alpheus, the whole story even about him wanting to divorce me quietly. Alpheus will be the only person who knows that part of the story. It would cause Joseph embarrassment for me to tell anyone else. That secret will remain in this journal and with Alpheus for eternity. Zechariah and Elizabeth know but they won't ever tell anyone.

Dear God, help me to be the wife You expect all women to be. As

You gave Eve to Adam as a helpmate, You have given me to Joseph. Give me the patience of Job as I wait for the promise of the angel when we can complete our union as husband and wife. Help me to cherish each day knowing that You have blessed me with a wonderful husband and child.

Mary's Wedding Night

In those days Caesar Augustus issued a decree that a census
should be taken of the entire Roman world.
(This was the first census that took place while Quirinius was governor of Syria.)
Luke 2:1-3

Mary Adjusts to Married Life

The first few months of married life have been somewhat chaotic, but I am finally adjusting. My vision of everything falling into place and Joseph and I living happily ever after, as I've always heard, did not exactly happen. Truthfully, I had a little difficulty fitting Joseph's schedule into my life. The first day Joseph came in from his shop expecting a noonday meal, it surprised me. His "What's this?" smile when I placed a loaf of bread and plate of honey in front of him, informed me that a man who works needs some hearty nourishment. He never says a word and never complains, but I think he had expectations of me being a little more domesticated.

My mother loved to cook and always began the meals while my sister and I studied or played. We helped, but the planning had already been done. Even when I stayed with Elizabeth and Zechariah, they did not have a certain schedule. Their eating habits were quite different from most people. Many meals we ate only bread and honey. As long as they had honey in their house, they were satisfied. Elizabeth did teach me how to cook many different vegetables and fish and lamb, but they didn't eat a lot of meat. My limited experience did not prepare me for Joseph's schedule. After the first surprise, I have gotten that time frame established and now have a meal prepared when he arrives.

Most girls my age already know how to cook and plan a meal, but since my parents allowed me to study, I sometimes forgot the cooking lesson. I will never forget my first attempt at cooking fish when the clouds of smoke forced Joseph to evacuate his shop. My cooking and planning skills have greatly improved since those initial experiences.

My weaving skills are also coming along nicely. With the guidance of our neighbor who is a skilled quilter, I am weaving a beautiful quilt for the cradle Joseph is finishing. It has not been easy, but I am enjoying every minute of it.

Elizabeth taught me some sewing skills. She stitched most of

Zechariah's priestly garments. The feel of the rich texture of those garments sent chills through my fingers as I worked on them. When Jesus receives his kingdom, will we wear garments made of the rich material?

My writing has not been as often as I hoped it would be these last few months since Joseph allows me to help in the shop. However, I fear those days may soon be coming to an end, because my belly is beginning to interfere with my work and my feet are starting to look like those balls the children play with in the street. When I bump into something or get too close to his cutting tools, Joseph smiles and directs me back into our room.

It is impossible to keep the house clean! The dust from Joseph's shop settles on everything and Droopy doesn't help much either. I decided that if the donkey was going to be a part of our family he needed a name. Droopy seemed to describe him very well. He has the longest droopy ears I have ever seen and even his face seems to droop. During the day I take Droopy outside so I can at least sweep the floor. Since he is our only means of transportation and does a lot of the heavy work for Joseph, we tether him in our room at night for his safety. He is treated like an important member of the family. Even more so, now that we have learned we must travel to Bethlehem to be counted for the census and pay our taxes.

We found out today that Emperor Caesar Augustus has ordered that all subjects must return to the cities of their fathers to be counted. Joseph's lineage is from Bethlehem. He talked to the local tax merchant and asked if I could be excused because of my condition. The man said all must go—even the lame and blind have to report. Some may even have to be carried. It has been years since the last census and Caesar wants to make sure everyone is counted (so they can pay the right amount of taxes, I am sure). He has no idea the hardship this will cause for most families and, furthermore, he doesn't care.

Joseph tried to console me by reminding me of the prophecies that the Messiah would be born in Bethlehem, but that only made me realize that my mother would not be there. I will have to do this all alone. I hate leaving Mother about the time my baby is due, but it doesn't worry me nearly as much as it would have before my visit to Elizabeth's. That time and experience with Elizabeth has eased many of my worries. If my birth is as easy as hers, I could probably deliver the baby by myself. She made it look so natural and easy. Wherever I am, I know my God will only be a prayer away.

Joseph also promised that if we timed the trip right and the weather cooperated, we would see the beautiful city of Jerusalem at sundown on the fifth day of our trip. I have often dreamed of viewing that great city at night with the lights stretching as far as the eye could see. Now it looks like it is finally going to happen. Poor Droopy will have to carry me most of the way. Riding on a donkey with my big belly does not sound like much fun. I wonder if a baby has ever bounced out of a womb.

It will be a long, dusty, crowded road to travel since everyone must go. I hope we can get there and register before our baby is born. Joseph said a baby would greatly increase our taxes and we can barely afford to pay them as is.

This little "king" I am carrying has been doing exercises in my stomach every night. Sometimes it seems there must be a dozen in there. He has to be playing with someone. Joseph saw my stomach moving last night. I took his hand and gently placed it where he could feel the movement. About that time, my baby started his daily routine. Joseph's smile stretched from ear to ear as he burst into laughter. He said the baby would be a good fighter with that powerful punch. Then he grew somber. His dark eyes searched my soul. He kissed me gently and again apologized for ever doubting me. Bless his heart. The feeling of guilt for thinking of sending me away when I first told him about the baby, still plagues him. The more I try to explain to him that it had to happen that way because God planned it, the worse he feels. I don't believe he will ever doubt me again.

He again kissed me on my forehead and then on my lips—this time with passion. I felt a surge of hunger rush from my body. I long to consummate our marriage, but Joseph promised I would remain a virgin until the baby is born and we will live with that decision. His body shows me that he wants me as badly as I want him. It took every ounce of our being to pull away from each other. He gently laid my head in his lap and patted my bulging belly. I laid there and longed for the ultimate bonding of our marriage. It will come, but I must be patient.

Dear God, thank You again for such a wonderful soul mate. He is my life now and I love him with all my heart. Give us the patience needed to wait for that ultimate bonding of husband and wife. Your prophets said the child shall be born of a virgin in Bethlehem. It now appears You have set plans into place for those prophecies to be fulfilled.

And everyone went to his own town to register.
Luke 2:1-3

Mary Prepares for the Trip to Bethlehem

I can only take the time to write a few words because there is still much to do before we leave. Since our traveling conditions will probably not be suitable for writing, I don't know when I will be able to write again.

We will leave early in the morning for the long trip to Bethlehem. It should take five or six days if everything goes as planned. My baby is due to arrive any time now. According to my estimates, he was conceived by the Holy Spirit nine months ago this time next week. My stomach is big and my body is telling me the time is soon. I'm starting to look exactly like Elizabeth right before John's birth. Joseph is still hoping we can register for our taxes before the baby is born. He says if we get there after the birth, our taxes would increase.

Though the road will be crowded, we will be traveling alone most of the way because we will have to take more rests than the others. I am not sure how much bouncing on Droopy I can take in one day. We will start out with one group and then join other groups as we stop to rest and others come alone. Since everyone must go, there will be a constant flow of travelers. One worry I have is the thieves who take advantage of people on the trail. If Joseph and I are alone, we are easy prey for the predators. Although there is danger, I know God will take care of us. After all, I am carrying His son, but that fact still will not find a resting place in my mind.

Everything is packed and ready including a few swaddling clothes. There is no room to carry much, since it must fit on Droopy with my belly. We will try to leave early to make some good time before the heat of the day. Hopefully when we get there we will be able to get a room to spend at least one night. We don't have money to stay any longer than that. I want to try to get back before my baby is born, but Joseph keeps reminding me of the prophecy of a Messiah being born in Bethlehem. I choose to ignore him, but I know that God has control of that situation and Joseph and I are content to follow His guidance.

A good night's rest would be wonderful, but I doubt if that will happen. All the pains and aches and swelling that women encounter when carrying a child have not made for good sleep companions. These last few months have been most uncomfortable.

The women in town are concerned that I have grown this big in such a few months. They think I have only been with child for six months when really it is closer to nine. They say I should not travel in my condition, but they tell me it is better to travel now instead of waiting until right before the birth. I smile and pat my bulging belly.

Dear God, please give me the strength to make this trip. Protect us and our baby and may we have a safe and blessed journey. As the time nears for the birth of this baby You have planted in me, I ask for the wisdom to make the right decisions regarding his care.

Mary's Praise to God

My dear heavenly Father,
You have blessed your humble servant
    and continue to bless me daily.

I know You have plans for me.
You have set me above all women by
    allowing me to carry Your son.

I will nurture him.
I will provide all his needs
    and feed him when he is hungry
    until You feed him what he needs
    to begin the journey You have already prepared for him.

You said he would be a king.
Will he wear a robe and a crown?
Will he be as smart as the scribes in the temple?
What unique abilities will he possess?

Will he be a leader or a follower?
Will he be as good a craftsman as Joseph?
What will be my place in his kingdom?

I have many questions that
    only You can answer.
Help me Lord to know the answers I need
    and to forget the questions that have no answers.

I trust You to lead me wherever I must go.
May Your hand be with us as we make
    this difficult but necessary journey
    to fulfill Your prophecy.

Only You know his every move
    I can only guess what the future holds
    for a child conceived by You.

So Joseph also went up from the town of Nazareth in Galilee to Judea, to Bethlehem the town of David, because he belonged to the house and line of David. He went there to register with Mary, who was expecting a child.
Luke 2:4-5

Mary and Joseph Travel to Bethlehem

I am fortunate to be able to bring this parchment and ink with me. We were forced to leave some other items at home, but Joseph is convinced that my writings are extremely important. He encourages me to write whenever I can. Since the fire still has a bright light and the ground is not a fitting bed partner with my belly, I will write a few lines to update the trip while Joseph sleeps.

The road is hot and dusty. From my view on top of Droopy I can only see the pebbles along the path and my dear Joseph who seems to have the worries of our lives strapped to his shoulders. This whole journey is also hard for him. At evening, he pulls the donkey away from the path and the river to keep the insects from disturbing our rest. My body cried to soak in the Jordan today, but Joseph was afraid it might be dangerous with some of the animals around. To soothe my aches, he wet some cloths in the river and brought them to me. The feel of the cool water was refreshing. Joseph walked this entire trip and he is concerned about me being tired. He is sweet and tender and considerate of my needs. What an excellent earthly father he will be to my son.

He keeps trying to console me by reminding me of the prophecies that our Messiah will be born in Bethlehem. The sharp pains I am having confirms that prophecy may come true. The memories of John's birth will have to see me through this. Although it seems I am alone, I know my God will not forsake the mother of His son. Whatever happens, I know Joseph and I will be able to manage with God's help.

We did have the luxury of stopping and eating in a home the other day. After traveling along the dusty road for many hours, we had about reached our limit. A man who lived in the area had been checking on some work. While traveling back home, he met us and took pity on our situation. He asked if we would like something to eat and to rest a few hours in his house. We were both relieved. To get off Droopy and actually rest on a comfortable mat for a while was a blessing. They also had the most wonderful roasted lamb and even some fresh vegetables. Everything tasted good since we have not eaten any real food after we left Nazareth. I wanted to stay the night, but Joseph reminded me that we were on a tight schedule. As it turned out, I am glad we moved on or we would not have been able to view the beautiful city of Jerusalem at sundown as Joseph had hoped.

I've seen Jerusalem before with my parents, but never at sundown with all the candles aglow. The city lights seemed to stretch as far as the eye could see. Being able to view the marvelous city while carrying God's son took on a special meaning. Someday his kingdom will save this city and return it to the Israelites.

We decided to stop and observe the beautiful scene. We were going to try to make it the rest of the way, but we were too tired and afraid we would not be able to find a room at this hour. The solitude of this place appealed to us much more than the crowded city streets. If we don't get there tomorrow, I fear Droopy will be my birthing bed. Joseph doesn't know the pains are coming regularly. He has enough to worry about.

We met some people today coming back from Bethlehem. They had been counted and had paid their taxes. They said the city had become one enormous mess. The inns were so crowded there were absolutely no rooms left. All the places to eat were running out of food and didn't know when they would have more because the crowded roads were preventing the caravans from traveling as quickly as usual. Caesar evidently had no idea how many people would be traveling to Jerusalem and Bethlehem. It has been many years since the last census and apparently, there has been a population explosion. When the travelers see that I am with child, they shake their heads and wish us good luck. Joseph is wearing a worried look these days.

Dear God, thank You for a safe trip and the good people we have met along the way. Help me, Father, to stay calm in this situation. I long for my mother's help, but I am content to let Joseph do whatever needs to be done. My body is telling me that my baby will arrive soon. Give me the wisdom and knowledge necessary to give birth to Your son I am carrying.

The shepherds said to one another, "Let's go to Bethlehem
and see this thing that has happened,
which the Lord has told us about."
Luke 2:6-20

Jesus is Born in Bethlehem and the Shepherds' Visit

My body is telling me I need rest and sleep, but I have witnessed a wonderful event that I must record. This good news needs to be shouted to the world and someday God will see that it is. For tonight, I will have to be content to record it.

What a grueling day! After a restless night and traveling the remaining distance from Jerusalem to Bethlehem, my baby told me we needed to find a room quickly. When we finally reached Bethlehem, we were overwhelmed by the crowd. Poor patient Joseph became exceedingly distressed as he searched and searched for a room. He knew of my pain and aches from riding poor Droopy. I knew my son was about to introduce himself to the world wherever we were.

Every time I made a sound, Joseph nearly panicked. The pains were so sharp and close together, I couldn't keep from groaning. He pleaded with the innkeeper to please find a room and a midwife for me. Shaking his head, the innkeeper pointed toward the cave where the animals were kept. "You can stay there for free," he said handing Joseph a torch to light our way. At that point, I welcomed any kind of privacy. In my heart I kept thinking that surely God would somehow provide a more suitable place. I couldn't believe that God would allow His son, our blessed Messiah, to be born in a stable full of dirty smelly animals. I also knew short of a miracle that no rooms were available, and God must also have a reason for even this. Being older and a little wiser, Joseph insisted this may be the only private area available in the entire city.

"Yes," he said with a nervous, but calm voice, "God's son may be born in a stable. But if that happens, it is something God has planned."

Joseph's faith clearly told him all was well. Mine could have been a little blurred by the pain. I wanted to insist we travel further, but my mind finally surrendered to the demands of my body. It didn't seem to matter to this precious little baby whether we were in a mansion or a stable. Remembering that God indeed is in charge, my fretting turned to instant peace with the undesirable situation. My mind accepted the fact that the circumstances God presented to us are only the beginning of Him fulfilling His prophecies—on His terms, not mine.

We wearily walked down the path to the cave being used for a stable. Joseph searched the walls until he found a place to hold the torch. As light flooded the darkness, I could see there were as many animals in the cave as there were people in the inn. I fought back the flood of tears slowly seeping from my eyes, as my thoughts turned to the inn floor which seemed to be a better alternative. At that point, Joseph spotted an empty stall full of fresh hay that had been boarded off from the animals. Adjusting the hay and shooing away any unwanted animals, he managed to make a decent bed. With Joseph's help I dismounted Droopy and lay down. Joseph turned to unpack our few belongings when my loud scream quickly drew him back because this baby was coming NOW!

As I laid on the hay with Joseph attending to my needs, I could hear all the animal sounds which almost seemed like they were singing. What an amazing sound as their usual animal noises were now blending in with the rhythm of the groans from my birth. Watching and listening to the animals, I forgot about the pain of the birth. The voice of the midwife who attended Elizabeth echoed in my mind. I obeyed her commands and pushed as hard as I could until my son finally arrived. He started crying and all the animals were silent for a brief second. The silence sounded more eerie than the noise. Then they all started "singing" at the top of their lungs. They were trying to harmonize with my baby's crying. Seeing the relief on Joseph's face, I patted his big strong hands and told him he could go unpack Droopy. He placed the baby at my bosom and left me to adore my precious bundle of joy.

The innkeeper's wife, hearing of my plight, sent some fresh water and some old cloths. Joseph tenderly cleaned the baby and me as much as possible. He retrieved the swaddling cloths from Droopy and wrapped the baby. I held my little Jesus in my arms as Joseph searched the stable for something to lay him in. Right in front of us stood a feeding trough for the animals. Joseph shook out the dust, put in some fresh hay and laid the baby in the makeshift cradle. I recalled the beautiful cradle Joseph had crafted for Elizabeth and the one he had made for us, still in our home in Nazareth.

The baby quietly laid there as Joseph and I sat on the hay admiring our handiwork. All of a sudden a bunch of shepherds stormed into the stable. My heart began racing wildly. Afraid they were going to take my baby, I struggled to get up and grab him, but Joseph eased me down with little effort. Then the strangest thing happened. The shepherds started bowing down before the manger. Even now, the memory brings tears of awe to my eyes.

"What are they doing?" I asked Joseph.

"They are worshipping their Savior," he calmly replied.

Then the shepherds proceeded to tell us their story. They were tending their sheep on a nearby hillside when a light shown brightly all around them. An angel appeared to them. They were sore afraid until the angel told them not to be, that he brought good news of great joy for everyone. The angel went on to say that in the town of David a Savior had been born who is Christ the Lord. The angel told them there would be a sign: You will find the baby wrapped in swaddling cloths lying in a manger. Then a great company of angels immediately appeared, praising God and singing, "Glory to God in the highest, and on earth peace, good will to men."

The shepherds said the angels disappeared as quickly as they had appeared. The shepherds wasted no time coming to Bethlehem to see what the angels were talking about. A bright star led them straight to this stable and, sure enough, there was the baby lying in a manger—exactly as the angels had told them. With much fear and amazement, I listened to what they had to say.

They were content to stare with eyes full of love and adoration at my tiny little baby boy. This scene in a chilly stable, warmed only by the animals and the bodies of the shepherds, is close to their hearts. They are used to living in similar conditions. They were delighted that God saw fit to send his Son to earth in an abode only slightly less worthy than their own homes in the hills. The shepherds are men of poverty and humility, but their adoration for my newborn baby came from overflowing hearts rich with devotion and love for their Messiah.

They knelt on the bare floor of the cave, staring at the ruddy face of my baby for some time. They were trying to etch in their memories this peaceful scene in the stable. The serenity of the animals gazing over the stall to view my baby whom, by the grace of God's caring hand, Joseph and I delivered, must have been a sight to behold.

The shepherds left, glorifying and praising God for all the things they had heard and seen. I, too, praise my Lord for sending them to us. I have stored their words in my heart, even as I commit them to this journal. Our king did not come on a cloud with trumpeting angels. He came as a tiny innocent baby surrounded only by the voices of God's animals. The stable became a mansion tonight. I became a queen and my son indeed became a glorious king.

As the shepherds left, I noticed that darkness no longer filled the entrance to the cave. The star they had followed shone brightly directly above the cave. I couldn't help but smile as I thought how God took care of our needs. In a lowly stable, Joseph and I are more blessed than King Herod in his glorious mansion.

It is truly a blessing to be able to record all this tonight; but, as tired as I am, I must stop and feed my baby. I am confident the strength I need to care for him will be provided. As I prepare for my precious little boy to feed from my breasts, I seep tears of pure joy filled with love, and, I confess, a little wonder of what lies ahead—especially after such an incredible beginning.

Dear God, thank You for guiding us through the delivery of my precious baby boy. I ask that you bestow upon me the ability to share him with the people You will send to worship and praise him. Fill me with wisdom to understand what I see and hear and to accept the things I will never understand.

When they had seen him, they spread the word concerning what had been told them about this child, and all who heard it were amazed at what the shepherds said to them.
Luke 2:17-20

Men's Reaction to the Shepherd's Story

Joseph and I decided to stay in Bethlehem for the eight days until Jesus' circumcision. It seems appropriate to have the deed performed in the holy temple of his father. Joseph scavenged around the inn until he found enough boards to make a room for us directly inside the doorway of the cave. To some extent it resembles our house in Nazareth. The animals are blocked out and we have plenty of hay for our bed. Jesus still sleeps in the manger unless he is snuggled up beside me. Usually when I feed him in the night, I leave his warm cuddly body lying beside me. In an improvised house in a lowly stable, I am still greatly blessed among women.

Crowds of people still swarm the city, but I am at home in this temporary house beside the adoring animals. Jesus and I sit outside the cave most of the day while Joseph works on various jobs for the innkeeper in exchange for food and clothes. I never realized how many changing cloths it takes to keep a little baby clean.

Since we must hold on to what little we have to pay our taxes, Joseph has become a master in the art of finding the supplies we need. It is amazing how resourceful a man can be when it comes to providing for his family. Most of the people are eager to help when they hear of our plight, but some only turn up their nose.

Today Jesus and I were sitting by the door of our "house" waiting for Joseph to return from his work. I overheard a group of men from the inn laughing about some shepherds who told a bizarre story about the birth of the Messiah. They were laughing at the shepherds for thinking they had actually witnessed something that great. It is easy to understand their disbelief. Shepherds are commonly considered untrustworthy. Many courts will not even permit their testimony in civil or criminal cases. I briefly wondered myself why the angels would appear to shepherds, until I saw their absolute love and total devotion when they visited that night. They unconditionally accepted the surroundings because it was close to their own lives.

As the men walked by, they pointed to us and laughed. "Could this be the savior those shepherds were talking about?" they mocked. "A virgin birth! Do these shepherds think they witnessed the birth of our Messiah in this stable to these poor people? I think maybe the husband should have a talk with some of his neighbors!"

Walking away, they leaned back, laughing and pointing. Joseph looked at me and smiled as he walked down the hill not far behind them. As long as Joseph and I know the truth, we will tolerate the sneers and doubts of others.

Today we finally went to be counted for the census and to pay our taxes. As we feared, the baby increased the amount due. We did not have enough to pay. Joseph looked worried, because men have been known to be thrown in jail for failure to pay their taxes. As we were waiting there, trying to decide what we should do, an elderly lady approached. She smiled and handed us the amount needed plus a little more. "God bless you and your baby," she said as she slipped through the crowd before we could even thank her. Joseph and I stood there and stared at each other. We've been doing that a lot lately.

Joseph paid our taxes with no questions asked. We were quietly apprehensive as I held our baby tightly to my bosom and Joseph slowly led us back down the path to our house in the cave. The darkness of the night allowed Joseph and me to see the brightly shining star that has been hanging above the cave ever since the shepherd's visit. It still lights up our entire room and most of the cave.

As inspiring as these events have been, I am still tired and weary of the hustle and bustle and the crowd in this little town of Bethlehem. Hopefully, we can return to the comfort of our house and families in Nazareth in a few days.

Who else are we to meet while we wait? What other troubles will we encounter? I know there will probably be many. I am also certain that whatever happens, God will provide us a means to resolve any problems we encounter.

Dear God, thank You for sending someone to take care of our taxes today. Even living in this crude house in the cave, You have richly blessed us. Help us to be Your vessel to pour out the truth for the world to know what You have freely given to everyone. Forgive those who don't believe our story. It *is* quite incredulous. Although it has been foretold, it is still difficult to believe that our Messiah could be born in such meager surroundings.

On the eighth day, when it was time to circumcise him, he was named Jesus,
the name the angel had given him before he had been conceived.
Luke 2:21; Matthew 1:25

Jesus is Circumcised

This makeshift house Joseph made for us has gotten a little smaller each day of the eight days we have been here. Even the greatest blessing in the world cannot erase this cloud of homesickness that hangs over my head. We could have moved up to the inn, but we do not have any extra funds and the innkeeper said we could stay here for free as long as we needed. This room, almost as big as the back room of our house, is quite sufficient. Droopy stays in the back of the cave with the rest of the animals. We probably have more living room than we do in Nazareth.

God continues to provide for our needs. The innkeeper is giving Joseph some odd jobs in exchange for food. It would be nice to have a few luxuries for the baby, but there is nothing we need. The animals seem to enjoy our company. Jesus rarely cries and when he does, the animals either completely ignore him or they all join him. It is sometimes humorous listening to them harmonize.

Today we had to take care of some important business that is required of male babies eight days after their birth. As God commanded Abraham to circumcise Isaac, Joseph must also follow those same orders. Although it is a requirement of God, I couldn't stand to think of my baby being hurt in any way. Joseph assured me that the baby would not feel the pain. It would only last for a brief second and then it would be over. Wealthy families sometimes have a big ceremony to celebrate this event, but we will be content to celebrate with the animals. We will have to be extremely careful in this stable to make sure an infection does not develop. Luckily the innkeeper's wife often brings clean cloths and plenty of water to cleanse Jesus' wound.

This morning I wrapped the baby warmly and gave him to Joseph to walk up the path past the inn. Our little king saw another glance of the world he has come to save. We arrived at the temple around midday. Since I am still considered ceremonially unclean, I am forbidden to touch anything sacred or go into the temple. Joseph took his precious charge to the priest and asked if he could assist in the circumcision of his first born. I can imagine the priest agreeing with a smile. I'm sure he has seen other anxious fathers who wanted to fulfill God's command, but were terrified at the thought.

I can picture the priest taking his strong steady hand and skillfully guiding Joseph's until the first few drops of precious blood were shed. The first tears of pain were also. At that time Joseph told the priest his name is to be Jesus. No one here knows us well enough to question the name as they did Elizabeth when she wanted to name her son John.

When the circumcision was completed, we walked the half-day journey back to our room in the stable. Today Jesus became an infant Jew; a son of the family of David. With pride, Joseph bragged that he had been able to help with the procedure. He patted Jesus' little bottom as he handed him back to me. What a wonderful earthly father Joseph is.

When I hold this baby in my arms and think about his birth, I can't help but wonder when something great is going to happen. When the angel told me he would be God's son, a king, I assumed he would be spared any pain. Evidently God wants His son to go through the same experiences and emotions as every other boy. Until I am aware of the requirements of a Messiah, I must treat him as an ordinary child.

Maybe that is another reason God chose me. He knew I would not be able to bestow him with gifts or any kind of special treatment. Although I have reasoned in my mind that God chose me because of my skill with a pen, I still have to question His choice at times. Anyone could have given birth to an ordinary baby. Jesus is normal in every sense of the word. Like all babies, he eats, he sleeps (but not as much as I would like for him to), he cries (but not a lot) and he dirties his changing cloths (more than I would like for him to). He peacefully falls asleep in his little manger as soon as I lay him down. Most babies are surrounded by slightly better surroundings than Jesus, but none are surrounded by any more love than he is.

Speaking of eating, he is starting to stir and must be getting hungry again. I must feed him before he outcries the animals. With his lungs, he will definitely be able to call all his people with a mighty kingly voice. As sundown approaches and I prepare to feed him, clouds are beginning to hide the bright light of the star that still provides such brightness to this otherwise dark, dreary room. It looks like there may be a storm tonight.

Dear God, forgive me if I still sometimes question why You chose me. If You saw my heart, you know I will do whatever You ask of me for I am truly Your servant. Help me prepare this child for the destiny You have already planned for Your son. I know You will show me the way I must go and what I must do with my baby. I eagerly await Your instructions.

Mary Sprains her Ankle

This has been one of those days I will long remember. A terrible storm blew up early last night. The thunder and lightening had all the animals in turmoil. The clouds had hidden the star and the stable was totally black. Forgetting for a moment what a good carpenter Joseph is, I feared the animals might tear down our walls. Getting up to put baby Jesus between us, but unable to see, I tripped over the manger. The sharp edge of a piece of wood cut my head as I twisted my ankle and fell. Blood gushed from the cut. When I screamed, Joseph panicked and jumped up, nearly tripping over me. Feeling the moisture on my forehead, he took Jesus out of the manger and nearly threw him into my arms as he took off towards the inn to find some help.

Joseph said the room at the inn was full of people watching a senet tournament in progress. He rushed in asking for a doctor to help his wife who had fallen and had blood gushing from her forehead. Amid many protests from his opponent, a middle aged man finally stood up from the table and grabbed his carrier. He followed Joseph as he promised to return another day to finish the game.

Carrying a bright torch into the cave entrance, the doctor briefly scanned our surroundings. Raising his eyebrows, he shook his head. "At least you have some privacy," he said. "There are many people sleeping out in the streets these days. I would like to get Caesar and make him come down here to see what a mess he has created. There is a much better way for him to do this. Everyone didn't have to come at once. They don't care about anyone as long as they are in their nice comfortable mansions collecting our taxes. If I could be king for only one day…"

Seeing the blood soaked cloth on my head, he forgot about his eagerness to correct the Roman rule, and rushed over to survey the damage. The bleeding had nearly stopped by the time he removed the cloth. The doctor said any cut on the head is going to bleed a lot. He rubbed some kind of ointment on the cut which nearly sent me through the roof of the cave. "It'll burn a little bit," he said sheepishly after he applied it. Eyeing Jesus laying in the manger, the man asked if this was the baby who had been born in the cave about a week ago, the one the shepherds were talking about. Unsure why this man would want to know, Joseph looked at me and simply replied, "Yes, he is."

The doctor said the cut should be watched for awhile. The ankle, however, had a bad sprain. It had already started turning black and blue and beginning to resemble my once bulging belly. My heart sank when he said to stay off it as much as possible for a few weeks to allow it to heal. I told him we were leaving for our home in Nazareth in a few days. He sorrowfully said that was out of the question unless I could ride on the donkey, carry my baby, and elevate my foot along the way. Seeing that picture in my mind, I reluctantly agreed that it didn't look like we would be going home anytime soon.

After washing the cut and applying some more ointment, he wrapped a clean cloth around my head and another one around my ankle. He promised to return in a few days to check on my injuries

The man said he had been a doctor for a few years. On the way home after a hard day's work, a friend had told him about the senet tournament. Welcoming a challenge, he had stopped to play a few games, but kept winning and couldn't quit. With his family waiting for him, he appreciated the diversion. His mouth flew open when I told him I enjoyed playing the game, but had not been able to for some time. As he left, he gave me some herbs for my pain which I haven't taken yet because Jesus is nursing. My mother always told us to be careful what we ate when nursing a baby, because everything we eat eventually ends up in the baby's body.

Joseph took a torch and escorted the doctor back to the inn. As I lay here in pain trying to sleep on the hay, I can only think of our home in Nazareth. If we can't leave soon, we will have to plan to stay for another month. As directed by Jewish law, we must present Jesus for the buying back ceremony and I must go through the purification ceremony. The first-born son of every Jewish family is reserved for God. He must be free of bodily blemishes and an acceptable sacrifice. On the thirty-first day or after, the father must first offer the male son to God. We thought we could do that when we returned to Nazareth, but it appears we will be able to present him in the temple in Jerusalem. Perhaps God has another reason for this delay.

Riding that donkey all the way back to Nazareth would not be good for my ankle. It would be much easier to stay, especially now that the innkeeper has given Joseph some work which gives us some means of buying supplies we need while we are here. Looks like this temporary house may become a permanent one for at least another month. I can sit here and care for Jesus as well as I can sit in our home in Nazareth. It is going to be a loooooooooooooooooooooooong month.

The innkeeper's wife heard of my accident and brought some food to us this morning. She said she wished she could give us a room, but there were no vacancies. We could stay in the stable if we would care for the animals. She promised to bring food in exchange for Joseph's work. He eagerly agreed to that. We are thankful for their hospitality, but I wonder what she is going to think when she realizes she let her Messiah sleep in a room in a stable instead of a room in her inn.

This morning Joseph rose early to find a stick for me to use as a cane. It is awkward trying to hold the cane in one hand and my baby in the other moving around this room. It is a good thing I don't have much to do.

I am going to miss my mother and father and our home this next month. Maybe I can find some means to send a note to them tomorrow to let them know we won't be coming home for at least another month. Surely with all these people crowding Bethlehem, someone will be going through Nazareth. I know my parents will be overwrought with worry.

Dear God, I know all things happen for a reason and I am content to wait here, but please help heal my injury. I want to return home as soon as possible. Thank You for sending the gracious doctor to attend to my needs. I know it is not a coincidence that he answered Joseph's call for help. Give me wisdom to know why You chose him and why this incident has occurred.

Mary Sends her Mother and Father a Letter

Dear Mother and Father,

I write this letter with much sorrow, but please don't worry. Joseph and I are safe and your beautiful little grandson, Jesus, is also. He arrived our first night in Bethlehem. Thankfully, he waited until we reached our destination.

We found a place to live for a few days, but it looks like our stay will have to be extended. During a storm last night, I got up to check on Jesus and tripped and sprained my ankle. I am fine, so don't worry.

A kind doctor came to attend to my needs and has recommended we stay at least three more weeks before trying to ride the donkey home.

Joseph and I decided that if we have to stay that long, we may as well stay to present Jesus at the temple in Jerusalem. I can go through my purification ceremony there also. You will be pleased to know that we were able to have Jesus circumcised on the eighth day in the beautiful temple.

The innkeeper has given Joseph some odd jobs in exchange for food and changing cloths for the baby. His wife supplied this writing parchment and some ink. We plan to send this note with a caravan that will be traveling to Nazareth within a few days. As I knew they would be, all of our needs have been met.

Please check on things at our house and let our neighbors know that it will be awhile before we return.

We long to see you and tell you all that has happened in the few days we have been here, but that will have to wait. In the meantime, know that we are enjoying our precious baby boy.

Love you with a special part of my heart,

Mary

Doctor Luke's Follow-up Visit

I knew God had a reason for sending this particular doctor, Luke, into our lives. Today I sat in the stable feeling sorry for myself with my foot propped up on a stool Joseph made. Joseph had gone to work for the innkeeper and Jesus slept soundly in the manger. Tears welled up in my eyes like an active volcano waiting to erupt. If this is the miraculous birth of our Messiah as the angel said and the shepherds proclaimed throughout the city, why hasn't someone come by to see if it is true? Why am I sitting here, with my baby lying in a manger in a dark dusty stable, surrounded only by animals?

As the tears started to seep from my eyes, Doctor Luke made a surprise visit to check on my cut and ankle. He said the cut had healed as well as could be expected, but I am lucky it wasn't any closer to my eye. Thankfully he did not try to rub on any more ointment. My colorful ankle, which still resembled my belly, did not show much improvement. He said I should stay off it as much as possible at least until the swelling went down—probably three or four weeks. I have Joseph's stool to elevate it while I am sitting.

Luke must be from a fairly wealthy family because he came in carrying a handmade senet board and pieces. Unless my father managed to "borrow" a game board from the scholars, we always had to draw one in the dirt and make our game pieces out of stones and sticks. Luke helped me move my prop to the front of the cave to take advantage of the sunlight. He didn't seem to want to go all the way outside where people could see us. I think he feared what people might think if they saw a woman play senet. Luckily the cave is set back from the beaten path and the only people who come by here are the ones checking on their animals. We sat on a rock and played a most enjoyable game of senet for an hour while Jesus lay in the manger watching us. What a welcome relief from staring at those cave walls for the last few days.

As we played, we talked. Doctor Luke had a genuine interest in our plight. He had heard the shepherds talking the other night and, like everyone else, had been skeptical. No one in the village believed their story. As the cloud cover lifted when he left the first night, he noticed that the bright star the shepherds were talking about pointed directly over this stable. Being an educated person he has read most of the prophecies and believes that a Messiah will be born in Bethlehem. He wanted to know more of my story.

After prayerfully contemplating the idea, I let him read what I had written that night. The story amazed him, but my writing amazed him even more. He wanted to know everything about the birth and the angel's visit. I told him everything that had happened except for the part about Joseph wanting to divorce me quietly. When I told him about my "visit" to help an elderly cousin whose husband, a priest, had been visited by an angel, he jumped up and began pacing up and down with his head in his hands.

"I know that story!" he exclaimed with his hands. "A few months ago, some priests were talking about an elderly priest who had been visited by an angel. The priest had been struck dumb until the circumcision of his son when he wrote that his name shall be "John."

Doctor Luke appeared astounded that our two births were connected. He had a keen awareness of things that were happening around him as they pertained to the prophecies. His remarkable ability to quote the scriptures that foretold of all these happenings greatly surprised me. His story amazed me as much as mine amazed him.

He quoted prophecies I had never heard, even quoting one about the bright star. The story had consumed his mind so much the last few days that he had to come back and talk to me. His visit wiped out any doubt I may have had of the angel's promise. I felt sorry for Doctor Luke because of his quandary over what he should do with all this knowledge. He believed my story, but didn't think he could safely tell anyone. For him to make this knowledge known would possibly bring harm to our family. Herod is the type of king who does not take kindly to someone else being referred to as king. He even had one of his own sons killed because of jealousy over his kingdom. Doctor Luke said he would write down all that I told him and maybe someday someone might be able to use it.

We became good friends during our game. As tempting as it sounded, I gracefully declined his invitation to go live with him, his wife and sons, and his parents. I knew Joseph would be uncomfortable living in Doctor Luke's house, especially since we could not pay him for his generosity.

His son Luke was five, Mark was three, and Micah was one. They lived in a modest house in the heart of the city. He said he had been a doctor for ten years, working close to the temple where he studies every chance he gets.

Of course, he would have badly beaten me at senet, but we never finished the game. As we talked and played, he eagerly showed me some advanced techniques for my moves. As much as I enjoy the game, I never cared if I won or lost. I liked to watch the men play and spend hours contemplating one move. I enjoyed the company of my opponent, which was usually my father, as much as I enjoyed the game. About the time Luke had the game won, he picked up the board and said he must go home. After helping me move back into our room, he left with a promise that he would return again to check on us and bring his game board.

Joseph couldn't understand why my spirits were so high when he returned from his work that night. It is amazing what a little kindness can do for someone who is confined as I am now. I will have to remember the good doctor's visit when I get home and spend time with some of the less fortunate in our village.

Dear Lord, thank You for Doctor Luke. He has revived my spirits and my hope. If he believes my story, maybe some day others will also. Since You have mapped out all these events by the prophets, why is it hard for people to believe? The fact that Doctor Luke wants to record these events for someone to use, fills me with an inner peace. I am not alone. For Joseph's and Jesus' sake, please help me keep this peace for the rest of our duration in this stable. I pray You have given me enough hope to get us home.

Mary's Visit with a Family from Nazareth

Today has been an exciting day. A couple from Nazareth, Hanna and Samuel, stopped by to see me. They arrived at the inn and recognized Joseph. He told them of our plight and our temporary house in the stable. I now understand a little how Elizabeth may have felt when she saw me, because my heart leapt for joy to see a familiar face. I jumped to my feet, and for an instant forgot about the sprain until I put all my weight on it. I am definitely not ready to take any lengthy walks.

What an enjoyable visit. They were surprised at our surroundings but impressed with the "house" Joseph built. Before the couple left Nazareth, Mother and Father visited them and asked if they would try to find out what happened to us. The letter I wrote telling mother of our delay had not yet reached her. Letters that have a long way to go are sometimes misplaced before they reach their destination. If Samuel and Hanna arrive home before my letter, I know their news will ease my mother's mind. She must be thinking the worse.

During their visit, Hannah held Jesus and rocked him to sleep after he showed off his cute little smile and ability to blow bubbles as he gooed at them. She commented how healthy he appeared for a premature baby. I explained that with all the bouncing on our donkey, he almost bounced out on the way here. Her fake laugh told me that the whole town would know of my six month pregancy within a few days of her return home. I can imagine the conversation around the well when she returns. Oh, well, this has not been the first time and will surely not be the last time I will be the subject of their conversation. Thank goodness God has given me the gift to ignore their idle gossip.

They left with a promise to tell Mother and Father how adorable their grandson is and that we would be back as soon as we presented Jesus in the temple. I told them about Doctor Luke, but I didn't tell them about our senet games. Hannah would have found that more disturbing than my premature birth. With her nose snarled up, I can see her telling the women now, "I always knew there was something strange about that girl!"

Doctor Luke came by today also. He has been back at least once a week for the last three weeks. He is such good company for me. I think I would have gone crazy sitting in this cave if he had not come into my life with his senet board. My father will be impressed with the noticeable improvement of my playing skills from watching Doctor Luke's techniques. Today he brought an even greater blessing in the form of a writing scroll long enough to hold many entries. He smiled and told me to thank our wonderful government. There were only a few pieces of the parchment left from what I brought from home. God always provides the material I need to keep recording.

Doctor Luke asked if he could come visit us when we returned to Nazareth to read some of the other entries I have written. He knows he is welcome at any time. God has indeed blessed my life through Doctor Luke.

Before Doctor Luke left, he respectfully picked Jesus up and gazed into his eyes for a moment searching for something. He carefully unwrapped the swaddling clothes, and gave Jesus a thorough examination with a clean report of health. He laughed as he said his surroundings had not stunted his growth at all.

My ankle is nearly healed. We should be able to go home as soon as we go through the purification process and consecrate Jesus in the temple. This cave is beginning to get a little small, but I know that I am still blessed among women. I still would not trade the experiences we have witnessed in this cave for any room in a mansion.

Doctor Luke must have told some of the women in the town about our predicament. At least two times a week someone has come by with fresh fruits, bread or clothes. One lady came by and took what clothes we had and washed them. It has been good to meet such nice helpful people. They are all curious about Jesus, but I have not felt comfortable sharing my story with any of them like I have Doctor Luke. I think a few are visiting more from curiosity or as a favor to the doctor than sincerity. He appears to be highly respected among the people. God is surely directing me as to whom I should reveal my story.

Dear God, thank You for the visit from neighbors from Nazareth. It is such a relief to know that my mother and father will finally know that we are well and will soon be home. Thank You also for sending Doctor Luke into our lives. He is truly a blessing. I know You have a purpose for him as You do me. My heart is telling me that our lives will surely meet again. We share a devotion to You and Your service that will keep our friendship alive. As we near the end of our stay in this temporary house, I beg for Your forgiveness when I sometimes feel sorry for myself. Forgive me when I question why these things are happening. I know it has all been a part of Your greater plan.

The Lord said to Moses, "Consecrate to me every firstborn male. Exodus 13:1-2
On the eighth day the boy is to be circumcised. Then the woman
must wait thirty-three days to be purified from her bleeding.
Leviticus 12:4
Luke 2:22-24; Leviticus 12:2-8; Exodus 13:1-12

Preparation for Presentation in the Temple

We have been in this cave for forty-one days and I am more than ready to go home. The only things I will miss are the visits from Doctor Luke. He came by yesterday to play one final game of senet. With his help and direction, I think I might be able to beat him, but we will never know because he always quits before the game is over. I think he feels it would hurt my feelings if I lost or *maybe* he is afraid I might win. I cannot wait to play a game with my father. He is going to be sorely surprised when I beat him on my own.

It has been hard staying in this house for such a length of time, but it would have been even harder trying to make the trip home. It is bad for Joseph to leave his carpentry shop for such a long time, but we had no choice. Joseph thinks it is a blessing to be here to present Jesus in the temple in Jerusalem. I can't recall which prophet foretold it, but Joseph is sure there is a prophecy about his presentation. My ankle is healed now and I am walking like nothing ever happened. A little kindness and a little homesickness have amazing healing powers.

This has been such a good bonding time for me and Jesus since I have had nothing to do but hold and nurture him. I really love bathing, feeding, changing, and cuddling him. Caring for his daily needs helps me think of him only as an infant needing maternal love and care. While holding him, I can easily forget the words of the angel about a king and his kingdom.

This house has gradually grown on me, but it has been hard to write here. If it had not been for the scroll Doctor Luke brought me, this entry would not be written. I would love to write every day, but I have had to keep it to a minimum. Jesus is constantly doing something new that is cute. It is sweet when the animals come and look into the door of our home to watch Jesus goo and wave his hands and feet. The animals appear to be laughing back at him.

When Jesus is asleep, Joseph and I have time to talk and contemplate all that has happened and all that we know must still happen. The future may be unknown, but we are content to enjoy each day as God finds fit to give us. We have never lost sight of the real mission of Jesus or of his destiny—of which we are not sure. These forty-one days have been unusual but happy for Joseph and me even in these most humble surroundings. Now we are ready to present him in the temple and I am ready for my purification.

Tomorrow we again travel to the temple in Jerusalem to take Jesus to be called Holy to the Lord as is written in the Law. I keep thinking that God will provide a more suitable sacrifice than the two young pigeons we can afford. We must offer one for the sin offering and one for the burnt offering. A lamb, the sacrifice of the wealthy, would be a more appropriate burnt offering for this king. I remember how God provided the ram for Abraham when he thought Isaac would be his sacrifice. Perhaps, I am expecting a similar miraculous happening to take place tomorrow.

I have faith that God's plan will provide that young lamb, but I will accept whatever He chooses. Although we can only afford the two pigeons, I believe our new son is rich beyond measure since God is his father. God will provide whatever we need and I must be ready and willing to accept His answer with open arms.

The end of my purification period brings a promise of fulfillment that Joseph and I have anticipated for a long time. I know he is as anxious as I am. It is hard to believe that I am still a virgin even though I do have a six week old baby. After the birth of Jesus, by law we had to wait for any sexual relations until the end of my purification.

I still sometimes think I dreamed about my visit from Gabriel and I truly am a crazy loose woman as some of the people in our village will think after Hannah goes back and tells of the news from her visit. As long as Joseph and I know the truth, I will not dwell on the gossip of idle minds.

I need to rest now. Tomorrow will be a busy day with the five-mile trip to Jerusalem. Then we must come back and prepare for our trip home. It will take Joseph a few days to break down our house and I must return all the things the innkeeper's wife has let me borrow. The innkeeper is really going to miss Joseph. He has worked diligently every day we have been here. Most of his wages have been used, but we have managed to save some items needed for the trip home. The innkeeper's wife has helped supply me with extra food and cloths. I will greatly miss the good company of her and all the animals.

Dear God, You have blessed me with a beautiful little boy and a loving and patient husband. Even this small cozy makeshift house has been a blessing. It has given me time to bond with Your son. Help me to not be disappointed with whatever Your answer is for the ceremonies tomorrow. I am truly Your servant and will do whatever You require of me. Give me the wisdom to know when You are talking to me.

When the time of their purification according to the Law of Moses had been completed,
Joseph and Mary took him to Jerusalem to present him to the Lord… Luke 2:22
Simeon took him in his arms and praised God…Luke 2:28
(Anna) gave thanks to God and spoke about the child…Luke 2:38
Luke 2:22-38; Leviticus 12:6-8

Jesus is Presented in the Temple

Today is another amazing day in my life long saga. I wish Mother or Salome or Elizabeth were here to share these unnerving events. Joseph, Jesus and I traveled the half-day trip to the magnificent temple this morning. Our time of purification according to the Law of Moses had been completed. It was also time to present Jesus to the Lord to obey the command that is written in the Law of the Lord "Every firstborn male is to be consecrated to the Lord."

As we passed through the eastern gate, we came to the Court of the Gentiles. We walked by the five foot high wall designed to keep the gentiles out of the temple. The inscriptions on the pillars in the wall warn all gentiles to come no further under penalty of death. The young lamb for the burnt sacrifice that I hoped would miraculously appear, did not. With our sixteen shekels we purchased two turtledoves. We could not afford the unblemished lamb for seventy-five shekels. Apparently God did not agree with the importance I had placed on the item to be sacrificed.

Going beyond the Outer Court we reached the Gate Beautiful sculpted with a relief of the city of Susa. What a glorious place for the public to worship. Entering through the Gate Beautiful we came to the Court of the Women. When I first heard of the name, I couldn't believe women had their own area in the temple, but it was named because women were forbidden to go beyond this area. In the four corners of the Court of Women were smaller courts with columns where the treasure chest for the voluntary offerings set. I wish I was wealthy enough to place a large offering in those chests.

We walked up the fifteen circular steps to the Nicanor Gate. There are no words to describe the splendor of this area. I felt small and insignificant walking through those giant gates with the elaborate designs until I looked down and saw in my arms the baby who would someday own a kingdom similar to this.

Joseph held Jesus as my purification ceremony was performed. I dropped my offering for the sacrifice into the huge trumpets standing in the Court of Women. The station men helped with the sacrifices and offerings. As the incense floated into the blue morning sky, the hymn of praise filled the old corridor. At this point, I am considered Levitically clean from my flow of blood, free of stain. What a wonderful feeling.

As we were walking through the temple courts, a righteous and devout man named Simeon peered into the cloths protecting our baby's face. He at once fell back, shielding his eyes. Everyone turned to look when he emitted a joyful cry. Joseph quickly looked into the cloths to see if he could determine why the man had reacted so. Sick with worry, I closed my eyes fearing the worst. Joseph nodded to assure me that all was well.

Someone in the crowd explained to us that Simeon was a righteous man. His longing for the promise of redemption by God was so poignant that the Holy Spirit had revealed to him that he would not die until he had been permitted to see the Messiah. For many years he often came to witness the presentation of male babies, waiting for the fulfillment of the promise. The Spirit had moved Simeon to go into the temple courts today. He took Jesus in his arms and with a voice much more powerful than his stature would suggest, he praised God. I stood captivated as Simeon sang his song. I have written the words as closely as I could remember. He said,

> "Sovereign Lord, as you have promised,
>   you can now dismiss your servant in peace.
> For my eyes have seen your salvation,
>   which you have prepared in the sight of all people,
> a light for revelation to the Gentiles
>   and for glory to your people Israel."

Joseph and I marveled at his words. I looked into the old man's moist eyes as he gently handed the baby back to Joseph. Then he turned to me with tear-filled eyes and blessed me by saying,

*"This child is destined
    to cause the falling
and rising of many in Israel,
    and to be a sign that will be spoken against,
so that the thought of many hearts will be revealed.
    And a sword will pierce your own soul too."*

My body buckled from the pain of the piercing sword. My first instinct was to take my baby in my arms and run out of the temple and keep running. Joseph gently put his strengthening arm around my shoulders. Joseph and I stood speechless at what Simeon said. Most of the people around us were amused at Simeon's reactions to our child.

Today the old man gave us a divine warning. For the first time, I realized that with the honor of raising this baby, I may also endure sorrow and tragedy. Instead of the perceived pleasant task of nurturing this infant in righteousness to do the will of his Father, for the first time, I now thought it may be the opposite. How did the old man know this and what exactly would pierce my soul? Everyone around us dismissed the words of the weary old man. I sensed they thought this particular baby born of a poor family could not possibly be the promised Messiah Simeon had been seeking.

In the next instant, an old woman emerged from the crowd dragging her legs slowly forward toward my baby. A man in the crowd bowed curtly to acknowledge the prophetess, Anna, from the tribe of Asher. He told us she had lived with her husband seven years and then lived as a widow for eighty-four years. She came to the temple every morning and evening, fasting and praying. Anna eased up beside Joseph, peeked through the cloths at Jesus and turned away giving praise to God. She left speaking about the child whom all was looking for to bring about the redemption of the Jews. Who were Anna and Simeon? How did they know these things about my child? Joseph and I again could only stare in amazement as the crowd around us walked away shaking their heads in disbelief.

Eager to perform the necessary ceremonies before something else happened, Joseph took the baby into the Court of the Priest to the Gate of the Firstborn for the redemption ceremony. I could only watch from the Court of Women. Every first-born child is, according to the

Law of Moses, God's property. No earlier than the thirty-first day after circumcision, the father must offer the male son to God. The priest examined our child and found him to be free of bodily blemishes. Joseph redeemed him with five shekels and two doves. Watching from a distance, I could only imagine the relief and pride on Joseph's face.

Joseph carried his precious charge back to the Court of Women where I joined them. We quickly left the temple. I stared at my baby to see if I could see any sign that would have moved the old man and woman so. I saw no radiance, no halo, only a little round baby face, dark ringlet hair, clear olive skin and red lips closed in sleep—only a tiny precious baby.

Outside the gates, Joseph lifted us on Droopy and assured me that these must be signs from God. Neither of us had much to say on the trip back to Bethlehem. In silence we contemplated the events in the temple. As we neared our makeshift house at dusk, the star shone even brighter directly above the cave. A cloud protected the Israelites when they fled Egypt. Would this star follow and protect us as we traveled back home?

The mystery of these signs today has surrounded me with a blanket of fear. Are there prophecies concerning these events? I don't recall any, but I haven't read *all* of the scriptures, either. Now I am even more eager to get back home and ask someone or else slip back into the synagogue and read them for myself.

I think that marvelous sign I hoped for last night happened twice today, but it wasn't in the form of an unblemished lamb. God never intended to give us a more suitable sacrifice. He wanted to assure us that we have the ultimate sacrifice. He also gave us a glimpse of the disbelief of the people. How will we ever convince anyone that this tiny baby is really the son of God, the Messiah we have all been seeking? My stomach turns when I think of the reaction of people to the miraculous signs.

Someday I will have to tell Jesus about the commotion he caused in the temple at only six weeks old. Fear of the unknown hangs like a cloud over my head as I think of what else may be in store for my precious baby boy who is now crying. I must stop and feed him as I review the day.

Dear God, I am glad I have a chance to write everything while I can remember it. You have given me many signs today. Some of which scare me to death. Forgive me for the fear I sometimes have of the unknown, because truly I know that I am a part of Your plan. My fears should be replaced with praise for the blessings You have generously given me. Help me cherish every single minute I have with my baby. My prayer is that You will give me time to enjoy him before You must take him.

Mary and Joseph Consummate their Marriage

After the long emotional day in the temple, we decided to wait a few days before starting back home. I'm glad we did. Last night after Jesus fell asleep in the manger which he is beginning to outgrow, Joseph pulled me close. He whispered, "Your days of purification are over". For an instant, I longed to be in our own home in Nazareth, but then I realized how fitting it would be to seal our marriage in this cave. Many memorable events have happened here in the last few weeks. It seemed appropriate to end it with this wonderful event and wonderful it was.

Oh, my! Never in all my dreams would I have expected it to be like this. Jesus is six weeks old and last night on a bed of straw in a lowly cave, Joseph and I finally become husband and wife in every sense of the word.

I have been anticipating this day for many months, and now I am glad we waited. Maybe it is because of the birth, but the union was easy and relaxed. I have heard other girls talk about this act, but none of them told of the sensation and wonderment.

When Joseph pulled me close, he kissed me with an overwhelming sense of desire. My body responded in kind. I felt as if I had suddenly been set free. Joseph, my dear Joseph, the most caring and gentle person I have ever known. He tenderly caressed my body, which eagerly responded to his touch. The desire I felt almost made me feel like a sinful woman. I am still in shock at how much more I have become a part of him. Tonight I experienced the true meaning of love. God made our bodies fit together perfectly. It seemed He had molded us as one. The sensation of the raging fire running through my body overwhelmed me. I knew my body would explode at any moment. Instead the fire slowly smoldered into a wonderful sense of fulfillment.

I know God has a reason for everything. The birth of His son by a virgin fulfilled the prophecies, but the union Joseph and I experienced because we waited until after the birth, and because I was still a virgin far exceeded any expectations I might have had. If I had still been with child, there is no way I could have felt the emotions for Joseph I felt last night. My body reacted to the freedom to explore all my intense desires without worrying that I might harm the baby in some way. Patience is such a wonderful virtue and I am glad Joseph has been blessed with a triple measure of it. I was patient because the Law required it; Joseph was patient because he wanted it to be special for us. He was right. Last night we felt God's master plan that only a man and woman in love can experience. As we lay there perfectly molded together, the bright light from the star seemed to fill the cave with a warm soft glow.

Thank you, dear God, for giving us the patience to wait for our ultimate bonding and the ability to totally enjoy what You created for a marriage between a man and a woman. You fashioned the union to meld completely and smoothly. The seed that sprouted today will require a lifetime of nourishment. Yes, I think we can spend a lifetime nourishing this seed.

After Jesus was born in Bethlehem in Judea, during the time of King Herod, Magi from the east came to Jerusalem and asked, "Where is the one who has been born king of the Jews? We saw his star in the east and have come to worship him."
Matthew 2:1-12

Magi from the East Visit Jesus

Joseph finally finished the last job he had begun for the innkeeper. Today I delightedly prepared for our trip home. Everything is done except tearing down our makeshift house which the innkeeper said we could leave. Knowing the way he is about money, he will probably rent it to some needy family.

As dusk began to descend on the cave, Jesus and I were sitting on the stool I had used as a foot prop watching Joseph make the final preparations for our trip when the strangest thing happened. Three royally dressed men came to our house. I assumed they were lost and asking for directions since we don't know any rich people who would be dressed like that. When they saw me and Jesus, they bowed on their knees to the bare cave floor and worshiped him like the shepherds had. My surprise did not quite equal the time the shepherds came, but it was still real.

I hugged my baby closer, afraid at first to let them see him. I thought they had come to take Jesus for their king, as a part of God's plan. When they started presenting him with expensive gifts, my fears turned to wonder. Thinking surely they must be in the wrong place, I asked them who they were looking for. They boldly said, "The one who has been born king of the Jews, which we have found. The star has guided us to the one we know is chosen by God to deliver mankind. We were compelled to follow the great bright star because our God told us in a vision that this child was the one that would be the king of the Jews."

Like the humble shepherds, they stared at the infant's face as if trying to etch it in their memories. Their knees under their elegant royal robes knelt on the bare floor the entire time of their visit. God has sent people from the lowliest to the highest to visit our son. Surely this is a sign that he has come to save all people.

Tears silently slipped from my eyes. Each day as Jesus grows, I want to forget all the things about his birth and let him be my baby boy. He is a special child, but I don't know what that means. I look for that mansion fit for a king that God promised Jesus and fear it at the same time. When I look around and see our meager surroundings, I wonder what and when all this is going to happen. This visit from the three kings jolts me back to reality. My child is special—he truly is God's son and a king. Why he is with such a poor family, I don't know. I fear that someone like these kings will come and take him away to go live in a big mansion with parents worthy of a king.

The three kings presented him with three wonderful gifts. The first king laid one box, filled with the most elegant gold, at Jesus' feet. Even in the dusk of the night, it sparkled like the bright star. The sight of it nearly took my breath away. The other gifts, frankincense and myrrh, were of such exquisite quality. I could not believe that all this now belonged to us. We were indeed on the level of royalty. For one brief moment, I wondered why God had not sent these gifts a few days earlier to provide means for us to purchase that unblemished lamb for the sacrifice that I had wanted. As quickly, I knew the answer. God had always intended for the offering to be the turtle doves of the poor families. The type of sacrifice doesn't matter to God; it is obeying His command that makes the difference. Has He sent His son to show the world the true meaning of the sacrifice?

The kings told us how they saw this extraordinarily bright star in the east and had been directed to follow it. They left their homes six weeks earlier, not knowing where their journey might lead them, only that they had to find the king where the bright star rested. They slept during the day and traveled at night so they could follow the star. They had gone to Solomon's temple in Jerusalem to ask one of the priests where the newborn king of the Jews was to be born. The kings told the priest they had seen the star and had come to worship their Savior. The priests then summoned many of the Sanhedrin who had asked many questions but were not able to tell the kings of any royal birth that had occurred. They remembered reading scriptures which said that Bethlehem would produce a ruler, a shepherd for the people Israel, but they had not heard of any such birth.

The magi thought that made sense since Bethlehem was only a half-day journey down the road. They pitched their tent to rest and wait for nighttime to follow the star to the house of their Savior in Bethlehem.

The high priest must have gone directly to King Herod, because he ordered the three kings to his palace that evening. Herod questioned the kings to determine the age of this newborn king. The kings said they had only noticed the star recently, but it could have been there for some time. Herod finally allowed them to leave with the promise that they would return and tell him where the new king lived. He wanted to come and worship him also.

I immediately thought, "My dear God! What will I do if Herod comes here?"

Returning to their camp, the kings traveled to the outskirts of Bethlehem and awaited until the star rose in the night sky and then followed it to our house.

As they followed the star through the town, they asked several people if a king had been born in their town. No one had heard of any such news. Reaching the inn, they stopped for some rest and refreshment. As they were discussing their plight, the innkeeper overheard them and told them about the baby in the makeshift house at the foot of the hill. They were a little puzzled when they were told it was in the stable. Nevertheless, they concluded that this must be the child they sought since no other child had been born. They pitched their tents, dressed for a visit to a king, and walked down the brightly lit hill to our house.

After their amazing visit, they were supposed to go back to Herod and let him know all the details, but they felt compelled to leave in another direction. They said God is telling them what to do and they were willing to obey his guidance. I could easily tell they were righteous and devout men. As they walked out of the cave, I heard one of them surprisingly ask, "Now, where is that star?" I wrapped Jesus against the night air and followed them out. They were right. It had served its purpose and now it had disappeared.

I wonder what King Herod will do now that he knows another king has been born. The angel said he would receive the throne of his father David. I never thought that Jesus might take over Herod's kingdom. How will such a young baby rule that mighty kingdom? I can't believe it will happen like this. It is hard to imagine what Herod might do. I remember how he murdered his own sons to keep them from taking his throne. If he would do that, what would he do to a king born to a poor family like us? I do believe God will take care of us. Were these gifts sent because God knew we were going to need some means for a quick escape? I don't believe God gave me His son to give to King Herod and I will fight that to the death. Until I know what God has in store for me, I will love, nurture and protect His child. My child.

It has been a trying day. I wonder what other things we will encounter because of this child, but I refuse to worry anymore. I believe with all my heart that God has plans for me and especially for Jesus. God's advice leads me in everything I do and I try hard to believe Joseph when he tells me the same. It is time to feed Jesus and put him to bed. We are ready to go home so this will probably be the last night in this stable. I want it to be special for me and Joseph. We have been through a lot in this little makeshift home. I am going to miss it.

Dear God, thank You for this incredible visit. You have supplied us with an abundance of wealth to use when we arrive home. We may even be able to purchase a bigger house for Your son. Please help us to be worthy of this great task You have given us. Help us to be alert and aware of the things You are providing us and to understand if You don't give the answer we desire. May Your cloud of protection cover us for our journey home.

An angel of the Lord appeared to Joseph in a dream. "Get up," he said,
take the child and his mother and escape to Egypt. Stay there until I
tell you, for Herod is going to search for the child to kill him."
Matthew 2:13-15

Joseph and Mary Flee into Egypt with Jesus

After finally calming down from the surprising visit of the eastern kings, Joseph and I went to bed to get some rest in order to wake up early to begin the return trip to Nazareth. Excitement ran through my veins to think that I would finally be able to show off my new baby and tell my mother about all the events that have happened in Bethlehem.

Except for the few details I told Hannah when she visited, I wonder if any other news of the birth in the stable or the angels appearing to the shepherds ever reached my mother. Would she have any idea that it might be me? She probably would not like the idea that her grandson had been born and has been living in a stable crowded with animals. News like that would probably travel pretty fast since there are many travelers, but I don't think many people knew of his birth. Evidently most people were like Doctor Luke and didn't believe the shepherd's story.

As has been happening a lot lately, our plans were abruptly changed. Joseph shook me awake in the middle of the night and said with a quivering voice, "We must go quickly."

By his tone, I knew something was wrong. Without the star, the darkness in the cave made it difficult getting everything ready. We disturbed the animals and they all woke up, but didn't make a lot of noise. They wanted to tell us good-bye. They are going to miss us and I am surely going to miss them.

When I started to ask why we were leaving early, Joseph placed a finger on my lips to silence me. Though curious, I trusted him completely. I packed up the remaining things and grabbed Jesus out of the manger that had been his bed for the last few weeks. Silently slipping through the animals who had allowed us to share their humble abode with few problems, we left our makeshift house and made our way up the hill to the road toward Egypt. As we quietly moved up the hill toward the road, Joseph said he had again been visited by the angel who had appeared agitated and commanded him to go quickly to Egypt.

Egypt? Why? We have no family in Egypt. The angel said that Herod had begun a search for the newborn king in order to take his life. We both wanted desperately to go home, but neither of us questioned what we should do. I hugged my bundle of joy close to my breast. I must wait even longer to show him to my parents.

It is hard to be away from home this long, especially with many exciting events to share. Now we must go even further away to save our precious baby's life. We are fleeing in order to save the life of an infant who has come to be the king and savior of all mankind. As foretold by Simeon, the tip of that sword pierced my heart; but nothing can take away the warmth of this helpless baby boy snuggling close as I constantly pray while riding along on Droopy.

As we trudge along the unfamiliar path, my heart yearns for a taste of home. I should be comparing baby tales with Elizabeth, not running from a crazy old king. I can't imagine someone evil enough to want to harm a poor innocent baby. God made everyone including Herod, but it is difficult for me to think of Herod as a child of God.

This will be a hard trip for us since we don't know the road and don't have a lot of supplies. What we have must be carried on Droopy along with Jesus and me and my journal. That doesn't leave a lot of room for changing cloths for Jesus. On this foreign road, we will have to search for the water holes to wash out the cloths. We have the gifts from the three kings, but we have no place to purchase any more supplies and, if we did, no way to carry anything else. We will have to manage with what God has provided which I know is enough to take care of our needs. Jesus' food is not a concern since he is still nursing. Joseph makes sure I eat well to get enough nourishment to properly feed Jesus. We have never gone a day without food, but sometimes I know God sent our meal.

One day when we first arrived at the cave, we didn't have any food. A stranger dropped by and gave us some roasted lamb and a piece of bread from the inn. The innkeeper told him about the little family who had been forced to stay in the cave after the birth of their child. He dropped it by and looked at the child. He seemed to be happy to help us. We thanked him and he left without saying a word.

God will continue to take care of our needs, but I am still waiting for that mansion that He will provide for His son, the king, to occupy. Will we have maids and servants to help care for our children? Will we have teachers to ensure they are properly educated and trained? I am not sure yet how to train a king but I am confident that God will show me what I need to know. For now, all I need to know is how to feed, sing lullabies, clean him when he is dirty and cuddle and love him with all my heart.

Dear God, please keep us safe as we continue on this foreign journey, but above all, help us be the parents You want us to be. You had a reason to choose us. Forgive me if I sometimes question what and why You are doing things. All the events that have happened thus far are different from what I expected. Help me to understand and know that these things are all a part of a higher plan that I do not control. Thank You for always providing the material and time I've needed to preserve all these events. As always, I remain your humble servant.

When Herod realized that he had been outwitted by the Magi, he was furious,
and he gave orders to kill all the boys in Bethlehem and its vicinity who were two
years old and under, in accordance with the time he had learned from the Magi.
Matthew 2:16-18

Mary Hears of the Death Decree
of the Two year old Boys

Today I believe is the worst day of my life. There are not enough tears to
wash away my grief and my guilt. My baby boy has also been showered
with thankful hugs and kisses. If Joseph had not been wise enough to
immediately obey the angel's commands, I dread to think what would
have happened.

After leaving the stable, we traveled toward Egypt for many days.
Fortunately, we had the gifts from the eastern kings to buy the supplies
we needed. Finally we crossed over into a small Egyptian village where
Joseph found a room in an inn. It wasn't nearly as crowded as Bethlehem
the night Jesus was born. We stayed there a few days while Joseph
searched for a small house. Using the gifts from the kings, we purchased
a house in a small village along the Egyptian coast of the Mediterranean
Sea. We didn't know how long we were going to stay here or even why
we were here. Not knowing was much easier than knowing.

A messenger came through Egypt proclaiming the horrible news.
Joseph and I could only stare in disbelief. King Herod sent soldiers
through all of Bethlehem and the surrounding land to kill all the boys
two years old and under. Had we not left when we did, Jesus would
have been killed. John would be, too. Did Herod's decree go that far
south? Zechariah and Elizabeth would be too old to get up and move
like we did. What would they do? Surely the angel also warned them
and showed them what to do. Doctor Luke also had a son one year old.
Did the soldiers spare the life of a doctor's son? Knowing the way Herod
operates, probably not. Surely the decree would not have gone as far
north as Nazareth where Joseph's brothers live or Capernaum where
Salome lives. When my mother hears the news she will be worried. She
knows we were staying in Bethlehem.

The messenger said soldiers were tearing babies from the arms of screaming mothers, throwing them on the floor and running swords through their tiny bodies. Even babies of the soldiers were being killed. Herod has even killed his youngest son to ensure no one would aspire to his throne.

I remember something like this in my studies of the prophet Jeremiah. I didn't know the meaning of the prophecy at the time, but I memorized it because I could feel the mother's pain. Jeremiah said:

"A cry was heard at Rama,
There was weeping and sore lament.
Rachel wept for her children;
She would not be consoled,
Because they were no more."

Thank God Joseph did not hesitate to follow the instructions of the angel. From what we can determine, the soldiers came through the day we left. Had Joseph not been willing to unconditionally obey the command, we would be mourning the death of our son.

Are we really the reason for the death of all those young babies? If so, why would Herod go as high as two years? Our son is only a few months old. I remember the kings said they told Herod that they didn't know exactly how long the bright star had been shinning in the sky before they saw it. Herod's astrologers could have told him it had been there a year. The way Herod does things; he would have chosen two years to be sure he killed the right baby.

This is such a devastating thought to live with. My heavy heart sinks to my feet. Poor Joseph. He is torn with grief. I keep thinking that because of this child, great things will happen. Instead, we have experienced much grief. Again the words of Simeon are truly piercing my heart and I feel there is still more to come.

Why would our loving and caring God allow something this tragic to happen? I know it has to be a part of his plan because every detail is specific. The three kings visited Herod telling him about the star. Herod knew enough of the prophecies to put all that together and order the decree. The three kings dodged Herod. The angel visited Joseph and ordered our hasty departure. We missed being a part of that decree by a few hours because of God's well-designed plan, but that is not a lot of comfort right now.

I am terrified of what our future may hold. For now, I humbly thank God for sparing this wonderful child. He is such a blessing and comfort to us and yet when I look at his beautiful innocent eyes, I can't help but wonder if he is truly the reason for all this tragedy. I want to cradle him in my arms for the rest of his life. I can't bear to think what his "kingship" may mean in future years. What is truly in store for him and us?

It looks like we will stay in Egypt for some time. We cannot go home as long as Herod is alive. He and everyone else would know that this child should have been slain with the rest of the young boys. He would order the command for it to be done. We must stay in a safe place to fulfill our obligation to protect this child from any more harm.

Dear God, please give me answers to all my questions and the wisdom to understand Your plan. It all seems harsh and cruel. Please comfort all the mothers and fathers of the slain children. Comfort Doctor Luke as he surely must have lost a son and would know that we are responsible. I can see him running to the cave to see if we are still there. Please help him understand when he learns this decree happened because of Jesus. Continue to keep us safe and secure under Your wings.

And so was fulfilled what the Lord had said through the prophet (Hosea 11:1):
"Out of Egypt I called my son." Matthew 2:15

Jesus' First Birthday in Egypt

Joseph found work as a carpenter in this alien land, but neither of us is comfortable here. My writing material is nearly gone. I must keep what few materials I have in case something miraculous happens. I also have to be careful that none of my writings are found. We are careful not to tell people we came from Bethlehem. They would know that Jesus should have been slain along with all the other male babies. News of Herod's terrible decree has spread throughout the world. I long to write Mother a letter, but I fear it might fall into the wrong hands. When she hears of Herod's decree, she will be sick with worry. I pray God will ease her mind and strengthen her faith to know that we are safe.

Although many years have passed since Egypt took the Israelites into slavery, I still have visions of them beating and forcing our people to work hard labor day after day. The villagers have tolerated Joseph and me being here, but they have not been overly friendly. At first Joseph had trouble finding work, but one neighbor finally gave him a job. He did such excellent work, he won over other villagers. Joseph's ability far exceeds the local carpenters. The elaborate craftsmanship of his work can now be spotted throughout the village.

Egypt would never be my pick of places to live, but I will always remember the time we spent here for the many accomplishments Jesus has completed during our stay. His grins and laughter are a godsend in an otherwise dreary environment. We were both delighted when, at five and a half months old, he crawled from me to Joseph. At eight months old to the day, a little white tooth popped through his upper gum. It took such a long time, I thought he would never have any. Then at eleven months, he took his first step. Joseph clapped and Jesus grinned from ear to ear with that one lonely tooth peeking out of his mouth. A few days ago he said his first word, "abba". It pleased Joseph when that little word came out of Jesus' mouth.

Today we celebrated his first birthday. We strived to make it a memorable day, but it is not the same without our families. From a piece of scrap wood, Joseph carved a little lion and lamb resting together. Jesus took them in his hand and stared at them for the longest time. He kept passing them from one hand to the other feeling the cuts in the wood. A few minutes later I looked around and couldn't find the toy. After searching throughout the house, we gave up. That night when I put Jesus to bed, the little figure rested under his covers. He took it in his hand and went right to sleep. It is still in his hand as I write this.

Jesus is a happy little boy even if he is a chosen child. I keep looking for signs that he is something more than most children, but I can't see anything. I still sometimes wonder if I didn't dream this whole story. I can't believe that this child will someday be the Messiah as the angel told me. There is nothing miraculous about Jesus. He is an average size boy with as much curiosity as a cat. The other day I was busy sewing, thinking Jesus was playing with his lion and lamb toy right beside me. I looked around and he wasn't there. He had crawled over to our low table, climbed on top of it, and stood in the middle of it laughing and clapping his hands.

Joseph is a wonderful father. He holds Jesus as much as he can, but with his work, he doesn't have much time. We still have some of the money from our gifts, but we spent most of it to purchase this house. We hope we will have enough time to sell the house when we return home, but, based on past experiences, we may not. Joseph works many hours to make sure we will have enough money to leave whenever we think it is safe. Joseph never mentions the visit from the angel or other events that have happened. By the way he looks at Jesus, it is evident that he too knows how special he really is. There is a glow in Jesus' eyes that sets him apart from all the others, but only Joseph and I can see it. My heart dances with joy when I watch the baby walk around the house, but I still fear things that must happen. Although I know God will take care of us and see us through the difficult times, I wish I could enjoy Jesus for the little boy I see now instead of what I know he must become. I cherish each day as I watch him grow.

Thank You, Father, for a wonderful first year. Even though we are in this alien country, we are still greatly blessed. Any loneliness that creeps into my mind from being far from family and friends disappears when I look at Jesus. My prayer is that we may soon return home and share this blessing with our families.

After Herod died, an angel of the Lord appeared in a dream to Joseph in
Egypt and said, "Get up, take the child and his mother and go to the land
of Israel, for those who were trying to take the child's life are dead."
So he got up, took the child and his mother and went to the land of Israel. But
when he heard that Archelaus was reigning in Judea in place of his father Herod,
he was afraid to go there. Having been warned in a dream, he withdrew to the
district of Galilee, and he went and lived in a town called Nazareth. So was
fulfilled what was said through the prophets: "He will be called a Nazarene."
Matthew 2:19-23

Joseph, Mary and Jesus Return to Nazareth

I sing praises to my dear Lord, who brought us safely home. What a relief to finally sit at my table and write this story. We had been in Egypt almost two years when the angel again visited Joseph and told him to get up and take the child and go back into the land of Israel, for those who sought our son's death are dead. Thankfully, we *did* have enough time to sell our house and the few meager belongings we had managed to purchase while we were there. Thinking, hoping that we would not live in Egypt for any length of time, we tried to live as simply as possible. The money we had provided a more pleasant ride home and maybe will provide a few luxuries for this home in Nazareth. We left as quickly as we could and headed home. My soul sang praises to think that I may soon see my mother and father.

The trip was a long lonely walk for Joseph. We could only travel a short distance each day with both Jesus and me riding Droopy. Joseph has walked a great distance for a child that isn't even his, but he could not love a child of his own lineage anymore than he loves Jesus. Joseph doesn't even realize how noble he is. He could still be living peacefully at home, escaping all the chaos of the events of these last few years. Does he think about other trials he will most likely endure all his remaining days for someone else's son? Or does he think about how unique he is to have been entrusted to raise God's son? When I look at him, I see why God chose him. Not many men would have completely surrendered to God's commands as he has.

At night we used some of our money to purchase lodging at inns along the way. It was nice to have a room for some private time to feed my toddler. My arms ached from holding him all day. Most of the time he sat in front of me on Droopy, but when he fell asleep, I had to hold him to keep him from falling off. My dear Joseph, who had walked all day, would rub my arms at night to bring back the circulation. Jesus always slept between us. I enjoyed the warmth and comfort of his body snuggled close to mine.

Along the trip, we had time to talk about what we will do when we return home. We are in agreement that this child will have as normal a life as possible unless another visit by an angel orders us to do otherwise. The holiness of this child cannot influence how we will raise and discipline him. I will begin teaching him the fundamental truths about God as required by law. It is hard for me to comprehend how I will teach him about God since he is God's son. Joseph and I reasoned that if God chose to allow him to be born in a stable, He would not expect miraculous things from him at an early age.

Joseph will teach him the skills of a carpenter. He will have daily chores of caring for and preparing Droopy for a day's work. When the time comes, we will enroll him in classes at the synagogue where the rabbi will begin a more advanced study.

Jesus is such a comfort to me because I can cuddle and feed him and sing lullabies to get him to sleep. I love my life right now and have no plans of ever doing anything else. I will always cherish this time God has given me with His son. In the synagogue, Simeon told me that a sword would pierce my heart, but nothing can take away the feeling of satisfaction when my precious little son smiled approvingly as I sang hymns and told stories as we bounced along on Droopy.

When we were almost to Bethlehem, Joseph talked to some travelers who told us more about Herod's death. They said that Archelaus, a son, reined over Judea in place of his father. Although the angel did not appear to Joseph again, he feared for our safety, especially Jesus. Afraid that if anyone saw Jesus they would report his age to the king, Joseph wisely decided to travel around Bethlehem and move north to Nazareth. Here, among our families, Jesus will be safe.

I wanted to stop in Bethlehem and visit Doctor Luke. I only pray he did not lose his youngest son in Herod's terrible decree. His visits were so enjoyable when he took care of my injury. Joseph and I both feared the risk would be too great. It would have been nice to play another game of senet with him. I am afraid I have lost all my new found skills before I even have a chance to show my father.

Everything that has happened this last year has been true to the prophecies. As a girl, when the priests were reading the scrolls in the synagogue, I often would slip inside, pretending to help my mother and listen to them. The words of the prophets Hosea and Jeremiah take on a different meaning when you actually live them. In my wildest dreams, I never would have thought I would be the one fulfilling those prophecies.

Although these events are terrifying, I know they must happen for the fulfillment of God's plan for His son...our king...our Messiah. I am patiently waiting for this kingdom to appear. Will it be grand? Will I be treated like a queen? Will servants wait on me? I wish I understood more what all these events and predictions mean. I tremble when I think how much prophecy has been fulfilled these last few years. I am not sure I fully understand the fulfillment of the other prophecies. I have difficulty understanding what God has in store for us.

When we finally arrived within sight of our home, Joseph and I burst into tears. I didn't realize how much I had missed that small house until I saw it again. A young boy who often came to visit Joseph in his shop ran to greet us. Knowing that he could run like a streak of lightening, I asked if he would please carry the news of our return to Mother and Father.

The house looked exactly like we had left it. My family and Joseph's family had been checking on things while we were gone. The cradle Joseph made for Jesus still set beside the oven. The blankets that I had made were lying in it— waiting for Jesus to come home. Joseph, lifting the sleeping toddler from my weary arms, tenderly laid him in his cradle. Tears welled in our eyes as Jesus smiled, grabbed the blanket and drifted off to a peaceful sleep. The poor child had to be as tired as we were. This room may be a little crowded with the addition of Jesus, but we will manage and we will be happy.

Relief covered Joseph's face as he lifted me off Droopy and whispered, "Welcome home, my love." My heart filled with love for the wonderful man God had given me and with happiness for the home and family we could now enjoy. It didn't take long to unload and unpack our few belongings. I know I saw Droopy smile when the last item was unpacked and Joseph tethered him to his pole.

The young boy must have flown to Mother and Father. They arrived shortly after we unpacked. What a glorious reunion. They gave me a big welcome hug, and then ran to the cradle to finally hold their new grandson. Careful not to waken him, Mother picked him up and cuddled him close to her bosom. She kissed him a thousand times as tears streamed down her cheek. "One kiss for each day you have been gone," she said.

Jesus did not sleep long with the tears falling on his face. I thought he might be afraid when he saw the strangers, but he smiled and gave Mother a big hug. He curiously looked around the room until he spied Joseph. Mother put Jesus down to watch him walk to his father. You would have thought he was the only baby to ever toddle across a room. Mother and Father could only stare and adore every move of their precious grandson.

We had much to talk about. They were amazed how the angel had warned us to go to Egypt. Father said it took a lot of encouragement, but he was able to convince Mother that God would protect His son. Father knew we were wise enough not to contact them to explain the situation. They prayed daily for our safe return. At the first sign of dusk, they returned home with a promise to return soon to hear the rest of our incredible journey. We insisted they stay the night, but they realized we were exhausted and needed rest more than talk.

Now that we are settling down, I will have more time to spend on my studies. I intend to go over each of the prophets again to prepare myself for the things that are to come. I also plan to start schooling Jesus. He is so smart; he may be teaching me.

I am also excited about starting the rest of our family. I hope the rest of my children are as good as Jesus is. I could not have asked for a more perfect baby. Even with all the chaos these first two years, he has made motherhood easy. Joseph and I were extremely careful while living in Egypt. With much uncertainty in our future, we did not feel comfortable conceiving another child. Since we are now home, I know Joseph will not feel the need to be careful anymore.

Dear God, thank You for granting a safe return home and a visit with Mother and Father. You have blessed us with an uneventful trip and have provided our every need here in Nazareth. It may not be a mansion, but compared to the stable and our meager home in Egypt, it is quite luxurious. Help us take care of Your child as You have planned.

Jesus' Second Birthday

This is the first time I have needed to write since we came home to Nazareth around three months ago. Our small house is a bit crowded, but we are so happy to be home we hardly notice. Jesus loves to sleep in his beautiful cradle. Mother said when she came to check on our house, she would pray that Jesus would be home before he grew too big to sleep in his father's handiwork.

Joseph stays in his shop most of the day and Jesus and I take Droopy for walks outside. It is surprising how quickly everything returned to normal. Even the women have forgotten that I supposedly had a six month baby. Hannah and Samuel have moved from Nazareth, and no one else has asked about the birth.

This week Jesus celebrated his second birthday with some friends and family. Even Judas and Salome were able to make the trip with their growing families. Mother now has six grandchildren counting Jesus. This is the first time I have seen Salome since my wedding and Judas months before that. We talked and laughed until my stomach and ears hurt. Thankfully, they stayed the nights with Mother and Father.

This is a special birthday because it is when children are to be weaned from nursing and pass through that uncertain stage of infancy. I haven't told a lot of people, but Jesus stopped taking my milk shortly after we arrived home. I didn't try to wean him while we were traveling because there were days when we didn't have food to feed him. Joseph made sure that I always had something to eat so I would have nourishment for Jesus, but I know there were days when he ate nothing but berries we found along the path. He is such a considerate man.

Elizabeth and Zechariah came and stayed a few days. The house was crowded, but the men and boys took their cots to the roof and slept while Elizabeth and I stayed inside. During the day, the boys played outside. Elizabeth and I talked for hours. They had also been warned by an angel of Herod's decree. Zechariah arranged for John to live with a group of righteous people who lived in the dessert. John stayed with the group until Herod's death and then they brought him home. Zechariah had narrowly escaped the sword of the soldiers. Apparently one of the soldiers had been told of the unique birth of the priest's son only a few months ago. When the soldier went to the temple to question Zechariah, he refused to tell the soldier of John's whereabouts. The soldier had his sword drawn, but was unable to pierce the righteous man knelt in prayer. Even the harshest soldier has a caring heart when God touches him.

Elizabeth was anxious to hear of our journey to Bethlehem and then to Egypt. Everything in Elizabeth's life is totally dictated by God. Talking with her, it is easy to see that she possesses the wisdom that comes with age.

It is getting hard for them to travel at their age with a two year old boy. They had never seen Jesus. They also visited with some other cousins. My sister Salome and her son John who is a little older than Jesus also came. Herod issued his decree shortly after John's birth. Thankfully he did not arrive early. Although the decree did not reach this far, everyone feared that Herod might change his mind and come again. He was such an evil man who enjoyed making people, especially the Jews, suffer.

Joseph's brother, Alpheus, his wife, Rachel, and two sons, Matthew and James, came from Tiberius along the Sea of Galilee. Four year old Matthew barely passed the age of the decree when the soldiers marched into their house demanding all the boys two years old or less. Alpheus said they looked at Matthew and let him go, but the sword had been drawn, ready to strike through him. If nothing existed to document the age of the boy, the soldiers were determining their age by their stature. The soldier's judgment decided if the child lived or died. I would hate to be those soldiers on the Day of Judgment!

I tried to tell Elizabeth everything that had happened to us since Jesus' birth, but she already knew most of it. With her knowledge of the scriptures and her wisdom, Elizabeth knew the people were talking of my child. When I told her of an event, she would smile and say, "I know. I heard Zechariah read all about it." I am amazed and bewildered. It is scary to think that events of my child's life have already been written.

News spread through the synagogue grapevine that shepherds were declaring that a king of the Jews had been born in a stable. She said the leaders were all shocked and scoffed at the idea. Zechariah reminded them of his encounter with the angels which they all knew about, but had chosen to forget. These leaders are not going to acknowledge that something good is going to happen to the Jews—especially from Nazareth. I sometimes think they enjoy the security this Roman rule has given them. The prophecy of the scriptures is not going to be fulfilled on their watch.

Elizabeth didn't remember reading any scripture about my injury or the doctor coming to take care of me, but she informed me that it did happen for a reason. Had we not been forced to stay in Bethlehem that last month, we would not have seen Simeon or Anna in the temple in Jerusalem. Also, she reminded me, the eastern kings had been following that star since the day it appeared to guide the shepherds. Something had to happen to keep us in that stable long enough for all these things to happen. The kind doctor was an added benefit, for now. I told her how Doctor Luke had taken notes of everything I told him. She smiled and in all her wisdom said, "There truly is a reason for that. Those notes will appear again someday."

My writings may go unnoticed, but surely I will have different stories to add to the prophecies. Maybe Doctor Luke's notes will receive some attention and the details of our Messiah's birth will be known.

As Elizabeth and I share baby stories, we realize John and Jesus are doing everything at about the same time. It is more like they are twins than cousins. It is hard to believe that these two boys have such important secrets in their lives.

Mother brought some of my early writings to me. I think she must have kept every piece I ever wrote. From my works, I relive the turmoil that existed for me as a young girl with the ability to read and write and play the men's games. I wanted to be able to read some of the scriptures in the synagogue, but only the boys were allowed. My heart yearned to read with some feeling and not as mere words like the priest did. I am attaching a few of my earlier writings in this journal to preserve them.

I was pleased that I could also announce that Jesus is going to have a brother or sister. When I told Joseph last week that I suspected I am again with child, he could not control his excitement. He danced me around the floor as Jesus chased after us screaming with delight. I must have become with child the week we returned to Nazareth. All the fear of an uncertain future disappeared the moment we arrived home. Joseph has been eager to start the rest of our family.

I didn't realize how strange it was, knowing the sex of Jesus before his birth. Salome once asked me how I could be certain that my baby would be a boy. If I had told her an angel told me, she would have only laughed. No one would have believed my story. It is really different not knowing. My mother and I both want a little daughter, but the boys are helpful with the carpentry business. Joseph would love to have a dozen sons, but I don't see that happening.

After such a tumultuous two years, God richly blessed us with a joyful celebration. Everyone enjoyed the heart warming scene of all the children playing together. Maybe I will add a little girl to the scene next year.

Thank You, dear God, for each day I have to nurture this son and relish in the joy that he has brought me. Help me be a good mother to all my children. Thank You for the visit with all the family and especially Elizabeth and Zechariah and John. They bring such encouragement that all is still right with You. Help me to prepare for the addition to our family and be worthy of all You have richly blessed us.

Mary's Early Poems

Child of God

My heart yearns to magnify my Lord
    in the synagogue along with the boys
    but I am not allowed.

I must read and write in silence,
    only my mother and father
    share my secret.

I want to fully worship my God
    openly, with outstretched arms
    and overflowing heart.

The love I have, cannot be contained
    within my soul.
It desires to break out and shout to the world
    that I, too, am human.

I also am a child of God.

He has blessed me with an undying love
    that cannot be quenched
    even if it cannot be shared.

Show me dear Lord
    what I can do to fully worship You.
Use me as a vessel full of
    love and devotion.

Help me break open that vessel
    so that love can be poured out
    for the world to know.

I am determined to worship You fully
  in body and soul my entire life.

I am your servant to be used
  any way you deem appropriate.

My desire is to spend the rest of my
  life as Your humble servant.

For I, too, am a precious child of God.

Womanhood

My dear God
    today I became a woman
    in every sense of the word.

I fear what this means—
    what will happen now.

As a young girl I followed You
    as closely as permitted
    even into the synagogue to hear the priests.

This Sabbath will be different.
I will worship with a renewed spirit,
    a newfound mature love
    for the God who has richly blessed me.

Womanhood...
What will it hold for me?

Will the young carpenter Joseph notice
    that I now have a more mature walk,
    a womanly glow about my body?

His inquiring glances have not gone unnoticed
    those tender eyes full of compassion
    his gentle smile melting my heart
    his long beautiful hair cascading around his shoulders.
But I cannot look!

Yet, I know he knows.
The accidental brush of his hand
    sends shivers up my spine.

As a woman my body prepares for babies.
May each have a special gift from God.
May they glorify my God as I long to.

My prayer is that You will bless this woman with
a compassionate and loving husband
and a house full of children
to share my love for You.

My Thirteenth Birthday

Today I celebrated thirteen years of life.
My lord has richly blessed me
    with a loving family
    wonderful friends
    and an enormous love for Him.

As a mature woman I search for a chance to
    serve Him as only a woman can.
My desire to proclaim my ability
    to read His words and write His songs
    can only be declared in secret.

The priests in the synagogue do not convey feelings.

Their words are mere words spoken without appreciation
    for the love with which the words were written.

The Psalms of David so full of his devotion
    become empty words when only spoken.
The prophecies of Isaiah so full of despair
    but always spoken with a remnant of hope.

The weeping of Jeremiah
    who sees much that will happen.
Why will Rachael weep for her children?
Why will they be no more?
What terrible fate must befall them?

Your servants loved doing Your work
    but Your priests cannot convey their adoration.
How are we to know Your love and compassion
    if we cannot hear it from the priests
    who read daily, but only read.

The emotion hidden in those blessed words
     wants to erupt—to be discovered.
Show me how to be the mountain
     from which it can be shouted!

I stand on the top with open lips
     that cannot be heard
     with outstretched arms
     that cannot be seen—a statue with feelings.

Break me open to allow my overflowing love
     to cascade down the mountainside
     to engulf all who are in its path.
Let them see through me the
     compassion of You.

Your humble servant I long to be for the rest of my life
A servant who can be used to the best of my ability
     not to sit silently while others proclaim Your glories.

I desire to use my abilities
I want to openly read and write
I want to openly play the men's games.

I want to proclaim what you have given me—
     the gift of comprehending the Psalms of David
     to know his pain and his devotion to You;
     The ability to show others of Your undying
     love and devotion for all Your children.

Use me Lord in a way that shows my undivided love for You.
Take my complete surrender for Your service.
I am but a woman unable to break the mold
     that surrounds the status quo.

Take all that I have and use me as only You know how.

Isn't this the carpenter's son? Isn't his mother's name Mary,
and aren't his brothers James, Joseph, Simon and Judas?
Matthew 12:46-47; 13:55-56; Mark 3:31-32; Luke 8:19-20

James is Born

Time has not been a friend to my writing, but I am trying to record the events I think God would want to be known. After we left Bethlehem, I had a difficult time finding parchment and time to write. Also, fear of who might see my writing prevented me from writing while we were in Egypt. If my writings fell into the hands of Herod, he would find out about my son. Now we are hopefully settled in Nazareth for a long time—especially since I now have two wonderful sons. Jesus will be three years old in a few months and James is one week old today. This birth was much different than my first one. Jesus' birth was quick and easy, but this one lasted for hours. When the midwife finally laid James at my bosom, I thought something terribly wrong had happened. His head was shaped like a cone instead of being round. A normal shape appeared within a few hours, but I was worried for awhile.

This pregnancy was as typical as my first one. The only difference is that Joseph was around to help console and care for me as Zechariah had Elizabeth during her morning sickness. When I had to abruptly leave the room, Joseph would bring me a damp cloth. He would stand and wring his hands until I was able to return to the room. I knew Joseph would be a loving and caring husband under normal circumstances.

God sent me an added blessing in the visit from my sister Salome who came to help with the birth. She brought her son, John, who served as a playmate to Jesus. She also announced she is about three months with her second child. I shutter to think what would have happened to John had they lived closer to Bethlehem. The memories of those young babies being murdered by Herod's soldiers constantly linger in my mind.

Salome's visit has been a welcome relief. They live in Capernaum and are usually only able to visit once a year during Passover. It is nice having someone with whom I am comfortable writing. When James is asleep, I have time to catch up on a few entries. We even tried to play a game of senet while the boys were outside playing. It wasn't quite as much fun playing in the dirt with rocks and stones for pieces as it was using the game board our father would sometimes borrow from the scholars in the synagogue, or the one Doctor Luke brought to our house in the cave. I amazed Salome with some of the advanced moves Doctor Luke taught me. She was surprised that he came and played the games with me while we were stranded in Bethlehem. Salome finally quit when my clumsy attempts to bend over and make a move resulted in more than one piece tumbling over.

We are both thankful for parents who believed in teaching their daughters. We have both vowed that our daughters, if we ever have any, will also be educated along with our boys. It is odd how we have had all boys. There hasn't been one granddaughter in our family yet. My mother is about to disown us.

Family has always been important to us. If Salome lived closer, the cousins would probably be best friends. It is good to be in a place that is close enough for my mother and father to visit. They visited about a month ago for a few days to help with the birth, but James, being a little stubborn, did not want to leave the comfort of my belly. Knowing the particulars regarding Jesus' birth, they are concerned about us and all that has happened. Of course they are the only ones beside Elizabeth and Zechariah who know the whole story. They know the scriptures and are overly concerned of what the future may hold for Jesus. Like me, they are not sure what to expect regarding some of those prophecies.

Jesus always greets them with a delighted squeal and arms opened wide as he runs to meet them the minute he sees them coming down the road. He will sit in their laps and listen to their stories for hours at a time. Adam and Eve in the Garden of Eden and, of course, Abraham are his favorite.

One day mother told him about Adam and Eve in the Garden of Eden when he added some details that I didn't even know. At three years old, his memory and comprehension is amazing. He told Mother where the trees were in the garden. She looked at me with a puzzled expression, but I could only shrug my shoulders. I have not gotten into that detail with him in any of my stories. Was he there with his heavenly Father? If so, the innocence of his three year old mind wants to tell what he knows.

After all the children were asleep one night, Father and I were able to enjoy a partial game of senet. He raised his eyebrows as I made some skillful moves. He did not like the idea that the doctor had visited often and had enjoyed playing senet with me. There is still that fear that someone will find out that I can play and it will cause problems for me. I still have difficulty understanding why there is a different set of rules for men and women regarding something as simple as a game.

Well, my writing time is over. James is beginning to stir and expects to be fed. He has the same lack of patience and healthy appetite as Jesus.

Dear God, thank You for blessing me with another son. Thank You for family and friends who are able and willing to help. Give me the ability to handle the two boys equally. Help me to not show favoritism to the one I know is special to You.

Jesus' Third Birthday and First Haircut

Today we celebrated Jesus' third birthday. At three, children are excited about everything. This is a great opportunity to introduce them to Judaism and the customs, traditions and celebrations that all generations have observed. As part of this birthday ceremony, we showered Jesus with candy, and then he licked a plate of honey shaped like the letters of the Hebrew alphabet. The birthday boy licks the honey to teach him that the words of the Torah are sweet like honey.

Then we gave Jesus his first haircut in our back yard. In the Jewish tradition, a man is compared to a tree. Since Jewish law prohibits a person from cutting down the fruits of a tree for the first three years of its life, there is a custom not to cut a boy's hair until after his third birthday. It is said that a child is like a sapling that must be fed and nourished. If you don't take care of it, it grows wild. Jesus is now expected to observe mitzvoth and the Jewish laws and customs. When time came to cut Jesus' hair, we invited each guest at the ceremony to take part in the occasion by cutting a lock of his hair.

Guests each took their turn, and the locks of Jesus' hair began to fall around him. A slight breeze picked up, and the large tree under which Jesus sat began to shed some of its leaves as well. God always finds a way to let us know that we are surrounded by his presence.

Jesus even made a short speech himself, explaining to the guests the connection between a Jewish man and a tree. Joseph had told him the story many times until Jesus could easily retell it to our company. The guests were amazed at Jesus' ability to recall the details. They all seemed to understand that Jesus too, if properly nourished and educated, might grow up to be as mighty, proud and beloved as a large tree. Jesus seemed to believe it also. At only three years old, he held everyone's attention.

James made his introduction to the family as he stole their hearts. He laughed and gooed at everyone. Jesus loves his little brother. Every time James cries, Jesus rushes over to see what is wrong. He always wants to hold him, but I have to be careful. I am afraid he would accidentally crush James as hard as he squeezes him.

Jesus and his cousins had such a good time playing leap frog, tag, marbles and some game with a ball that Matthew had brought. Joseph made Jesus a wooden game board. The pieces were carved from scrap material in his shop. I think Jesus may be a little young to play senet, but Joseph is sure that Jesus will be able to beat anyone in a game of draughts within a few weeks. Now Salome and I will not have to draw our game in the ground.

The older boys were eager to play with the new board. It is really a blessing having someone who is able to make things that are usually reserved for the wealthier people. I wanted to play a game with Father, but he and Mother did not stay very long. Mother said he had been feeling bad for awhile. They started not to come, but did not want to disappoint Jesus. He is having great difficulty breathing and tires so quickly. As much as Father enjoys walking, they brought their donkey in case Father could not walk all the way. It deeply saddens me to see him in this condition.

Dear God, thank You for a wonderful day with family and friends. As we watch Jesus grow and begin to observe the Jewish customs, I pray that You will guide us in what we should teach him. He is a bright child whom I know will learn quickly. If it be Your will, please help my father regain his health.

If a man dies, will he live again?
Job 14:14

Father's Death

I am engulfed in a shroud of sorrow.
Father has gone to live with his heavenly father.
I will see him on this earth no more.

Death should be a blessed event.
We are living to die, aren't we?
Then why am I in such sorrow?

God made birth and death
    to be events of rejoicing.
Why do tears flow from my eyes?

Am I so selfish that I would deny
    Father this everlasting peace?
Why do I want his aged body, writhing in pain,
    to remain on earth to suffer more?

My mind says "Rejoice."
My soul says "Set him free."
My heart says "Please don't take him.
    I am not finished with him."

I have a promised kingdom for him to see.
I have more children for him to love.
I need his strength and his wisdom
    which God generously grants him.

Life is so hard for the living among the dead.

"Aren't all his sisters with us?"
Matthew 13:56

Elizabeth is Born

Our lives have been completely normal since I last wrote on Jesus' third birthday. I have been busy with Jesus and James and helping with Joseph's work. His outstanding skills have resulted in many custom orders from some wealthy men. These orders are good, because when I am nearly out of parchment, Joseph will take payment in writing materials and ink. The wealthy have access to some items that are not readily available to our class. He had a large order a few months ago that nearly killed all four of us trying to get it done. Even James carried lumber and helped. Jesus, at five, is showing skills of a craftsman also. Who knows? He may become a skilled craftsman like his father. I wish, but in my heart I know that is not going to happen.

I still watch every day for a sign that would make Jesus different from all the other children, but, he is like the other boys his age. The only difference I've noticed is that he does not throw temper tantrums like his brother. Jesus is the one who gives in and lets James have any thing he wants. He is loving and caring toward his little brother. I hope he is as much with his little sister, Elizabeth, who entered this world only three days ago. Yes, I finally received my darling little girl and my delighted mother now has a granddaughter.

Another boy would have been acceptable, but God did answer Mother's prayer and has truly blessed me with an adorable little curly headed brown-eyed girl. We named her Elizabeth after my dear cousin hoping she will be as beautiful and gentle-spirited.

Elizabeth is often on my mind as I think about her caring for John. It is hard with three, but I am younger and have much more energy. I pray she is doing well and John is not any trouble for them. The last time we saw them, John had to do everything his way and didn't listen to anyone else. He wasn't bad, but a little headstrong. Hopefully that will change with age.

John and Jesus played well together the last time they were here. It really amazes me that they are so different, yet very much alike. They were trying to study and learn from each other. Jesus climbed trees and hunted frogs with John for awhile and then John would play draughts with Jesus for awhile. They are both good at the game playing. I want to start teaching Jesus senet in the near future. It will be fun having someone around to play with again. I have only played one game with my father since I learned so much from Doctor Luke. The game with Salome doesn't count. We laughed more than we played that day.

There is such a difference in the manner of the baby boys and the baby girls. The boys were always eager when they nursed. They had to finish as soon as possible because something else was always calling—even if it was only sleeping. Elizabeth lays there and nurses until she falls asleep. No hurry. If I didn't have other things to do, I think she would nurse all day and be happy. She must get on a better schedule or I will be sorry when my company leaves.

I only have time to write today because Alpheus and his family have come to visit and help with the boys. There is much work to be done for two growing boys and a young baby. I am thankful for the relatives who have come and given me a few days to really enjoy each new child. It seems our house would be crowded with the extra family, but they only stay a day or two and Rachel is such a good help with the cooking and house work. Jesus and James love to have company because all the men go up on the roof to sleep at night. It is also good that they have sons to play with my boys. The cousins have always loved playing together, and they truly do play like cousins. I can hear them fighting over something one minute and the next they are all playing together like nothing happened. Rachel has been a wonderful help, but she is not as much company as Salome.

Next week my mother is planning on coming to stay a few weeks to spend time with her only granddaughter. She seems lonely since Father's death. When a husband and wife have a good, happy life together, losing one is like having your life torn into. Mother crashed after devoting her entire day for many weeks to taking care of his needs. Father grew more and more sedentary as his breathing became more difficult. I could not help because they thought whatever he had might be contagious and could harm my baby in some way. At the end, we were praying for a blessed death and a release from his suffering. Death can sometimes be such a blessing. My only regret is that he will never see his precious little granddaughter. I really miss him at times like these.

I have to go. Elizabeth is ready for her next feeding marathon.

Dear God, thank You for this precious little baby girl and the time I have had to enjoy her. I especially thank You for Rachel's help. I pray Mother will have an enjoyable time playing with her little granddaughter. May this new life offer her comfort for the loved one she has lost. My prayer is that I will be a good mother to all my children and treat them equally.

John's Sixth Birthday

The last few days have been busy, but enjoyable for us. Joseph, Jesus, James, Elizabeth and I went to see Elizabeth, Zechariah and John after we celebrated the Passover in Jerusalem. While we were there, we celebrated John's sixth birthday. I am glad we took the time to go see them, because with another baby on the way, I am sure we will not be able to make this trip many more times. I don't think Elizabeth will ever be able to make the trip to visit us again. Joseph hated to leave his shop, but we agreed Elizabeth needed to see her namesake. Cousin Elizabeth had the toddler either wrapped in her arms or was telling her stories the entire time we were there.

One day during our visit, Joseph and I traveled to Bethlehem to see if we could find Doctor Luke. I wanted to thank him again for his wonderful blessings during our time in the cave, but we could not locate him. The innkeeper and his wife were still there and told us of Doctor Luke's story. They wondered why we left in such a hurry that day. They said the soldiers came through the very day we left and slashed the throat of all the young male babies in the town. Doctor Luke, attempting to save the life of his child, jumped in front of the soldier's sword. Unable or unwilling to stop the drawn sword, the soldier pierced Doctor Luke and his son. The mother was devastated. She and the rest of the family quickly moved somewhere north of Jerusalem. They asked if our son had escaped. I quickly said, "He is not with us."

I was glad Jesus had stayed with Zechariah that day. At first he wanted to see his birthplace, but I had a sense that he should not accompany us. It was easy to convince him to stay and play with John. As fond of money as the innkeeper is, I tremble to think what he might do if he thought Jesus had escaped the soldier's sword.

We revisited the cave, which was exactly like it was six years ago except the "house" Joseph made for us had been torn down. My body trembled when I walked into that cave and the memories flooded my mind. It is hard to believe such royal events took place in that lowly dwelling. We left quickly and have no intention of going back.

Zechariah and Elizabeth worked hard to make us feel welcome. Age may have been a factor, but Elizabeth never completely regained her health after John's birth. Her movements through her house remind me of a turtle on a mission. One thing is all she can manage at a time. She eagerly agreed to let me prepare the meals while she babysat with baby Elizabeth. This worked out well because I fixed the meals on a regular schedule with food to go with the honey.

Elizabeth needs much patience with John. I can tell he is going to be a little rebel. Everything he does is different. Jesus laughs at him all the time for some of the tales he tells. And he will not wear anything on his feet. Elizabeth says he goes barefoot all the time. He also will not wear the tunics the other boys wear. His skin is a golden brown from being baked by the sun day after day. His hair is long and scraggly and desperately in need of some care. Raising him as a Nazarite, his parents vowed not to cut his hair, but it didn't look like it had even been combed for days. If there is a different way to do something, John will find it. Elizabeth and Zechariah are enjoying his free will now, but I hope he does not bring them shame later. They let him do mostly whatever he wants.

John and Jesus are both such bright boys who never cease to amaze me with some of the scripture they can recite. I overheard Jesus and John talking about their studies and how much they loved memorizing the old laws. They feel compelled to learn as many as they can. At six years old, they can recite more scripture than most of the priests. Jesus has recited things I haven't even taught him yet. How does he know them?

I wonder if they understand what they are saying. They were talking like adults about some of the old laws with comprehension well beyond their years. As I listen to them, I can't help but think that someday God is going to come to take His son from me to start His heavenly kingdom. The thought scares me and rips my heart apart, but Joseph and I know we must be willing to give him back. I have a hard time picturing this humble and compassionate little boy as a king. He has none of the ordinary characteristics of any king we have known. I often think that Jesus' loving heart must be similar to the great King David. I pray we will know when the time comes for his great kingdom and that we will have enough faith to do what we must do. God will help us, because He would not have chosen us if He thought we would interfere with His wishes.

What a wonderful birthday celebration we had. When the women in the village knew Elizabeth had company, one of them baked a sweet cake for John and all the rest prepared a feast. It is comforting to see the women of the town taking such good care of Elizabeth. They know how hard it is for her and they are constantly bringing food for them. Elizabeth still keeps a pot of honey on her table for John, who must have it with every meal he eats. They rarely fix meat, since John won't eat it anyway. He eats vegetables, honey and bread. Jesus told me that John has also eaten some of the wild locusts, but I chose to ignore that.

She and Zechariah look old and tired. I wanted to tell them that if anything happened, please let John come live with us. Although I will soon have four, we would make room and Jesus would love his company. I think Elizabeth would want that also, but Zechariah would want John to live with the group called the Essenes who live in the desert. John sometimes spends weeks at a time there. When I first heard the priests talk about the group, I became curious and tried to find out more. I learned that the nonviolent group opposes the slaughter of animals in the Jerusalem temple and even has women disciples. The priests were worried that the group would become a powerful religious influence and a woman might actually have a chance to read in the temple.

Dear God, I pray You will care for Elizabeth and Zechariah and keep them healthy enough to raise John. I know that caring for a headstrong young boy is difficult for them, but I also know they would not trade their circumstances for anything. They are happy and fulfilled now. You have truly blessed them as You have blessed us, and You have especially blessed us for allowing this visit.

Isn't this the carpenter's son? Isn't his mother's name Mary,
and aren't his brothers James, Joseph, Simon and Judas?
Matthew 12:46-47; 13:55-56; Mark 3:31-32; Luke 8:19-20

Joseph is Born

Again, I have company to assist with the children which allows me time
to write a few notes to catch up on things. Two days ago I gave birth to
my beautiful fourth child who is lying here beside me as I write. Unlike
James, he has a perfectly round head as a result of a quick and easy
birth.

We named this baby after his father. I don't know why we did not
do that with James. Usually the first son takes the name of his father,
but in my case I didn't have an option since the angel, Gabriel, told me
what to name my firstborn. With James we didn't even think about it.
It pleased Joseph to finally have a namesake. I only hope he is as gentle-
spirited as his father.

Elizabeth has become a beautiful little girl. She is definitely all girl.
I have nicknamed her "Miss Cleopatra" for the beautiful queen whose
stories have spread throughout the country. Elizabeth dances around
the house in any kind of elegant material she can find. It may be a linen
cloth or a soft piece of scrap material. Our seamstress in the town used
to live close by and always gave Elizabeth her fancy scrap pieces. When
I find some time to sew, I plan to make her a fancy dress outfit like the
girls who dance for the kings. Joseph and her brothers don't really care
for her doing that, but I think it is quite harmless—especially at this
age. Her favorite toy is a little handmade doll wearing a fancy dress that
the seamstress made for her. Thank God for good friends. I would never
have been able to give her something that nice, but I can mend it when it
gets torn. That sometimes happens when James chooses to tease her by
snatching it and running away.

James is the shadow of his bigger brother. Thank goodness. Because
when Jesus is not with him, he is a little wild child. He does not play
nearly as well with his sister as Jesus does. All the other boys play with
him as long as Jesus is around, but he won't even go outside and play
unless Jesus is there to go with him. His schooling has started and he is
also bright like Jesus, but he doesn't like it nearly as well. I could teach

Jesus for hours and hours, but after one hour, James is in some other land being a king or a pirate. His mind is not on his lessons.

Jesus is kind and compassionate and patient, like Joseph. I think Joseph must be another reason God chose me for this child. Joseph has all the qualities of a great man. He is probably as close to our heavenly Father as any of the priests who devote their entire life studying Him. He adores all his children and each night after a long hard day's work, he still takes time to tell them a story before they go to sleep. Unlike me, who sometimes grows a little impatient when James is teasing his little sister, Joseph never raises his voice at any of them. His voice is always calm and peaceful, but authoritative. They know that when he says something, they must do it. No questions asked. Joseph says I am too soft with them as he winks and passes me an understanding smile. He knows that being with them all day is different than coming home to eat with them and tell them a story.

Jesus has learned from one of the merchants in town how to operate a loom. The other day he made a piece to go on our dusty floor, but it looked much better on my table. He and our neighbor Jacob are also great friends of the potter who works near the flowing spring. As they watch Jorum's deft fingers mold the clay on the potter's wheel, they both vow to be potters when they grow up. Jorum is fond of the boys and often gives them clay to play with, seeking to stimulate their creative imaginations by suggesting competitive efforts in modeling various objects and animals.

When Jesus is not studying or with his neighbor friend, he helps Joseph in his shop. Joseph says he is an excellent craftsman for his age. He smiles at me when he says Jesus will become a craftsman like his father. We both know that is not going to happen, but until we are told differently, we have to make Jesus think his life is going to be like all the rest of the boys. I am still expecting that kingdom and the mansion, but maybe he must wait until he reaches the age of accountability which is thirteen. We must be patient until that time comes. We have an ordinary family. We are not poor, but we are by no means rich. Joseph makes enough for us to live comfortably with not many luxuries. We are in every sense of the word an average family. Which begs the question "Why us?" Maybe I will someday know the answer.

My beautiful darling baby is stirring now. I must feed him. His appetite is as hardy as both Jesus and James. I am glad I weaned Elizabeth before he arrived. It hasn't been too long ago that she still nursed at night.

Dear God, thank You for another beautiful little baby. In my busyness with my growing family, please don't let me miss any of the signs You continually give me. I pray that You will not let me forget my role in Jesus' life.

And the child grew and became strong;
he was filled with wisdom, and the grace of God was upon him.
Luke 2:40

Jesus at Seven

This move to a bigger house is about to kill me. I know I have not written since Joseph's birth, but I haven't had any spare time. Joseph had been looking for a bigger house for some time since the five of us were about to pop out of our other one. He could build a new house, but he lovingly looks at me and says he doesn't have the time.

One of Joseph' kinsmen built and lived in this house until his death. At one time he had a wife, but after being accused of adultery, she ran off right after I gave birth to Elizabeth. If she had not left, she would have surely been stoned to death. The man and his father-in-law built the house to share. It is really two houses in one. Since the in-laws were too embarrassed to move in, half the house is like new. I think the poor man grieved himself to death. Joseph attained the property, being the only kinsman redeemer who would accept it. I feel sorry for the incident, but we surely received a blessing.

The house is close enough to our other one that the children can still have their same friends and can make some new ones here. Elizabeth cried when she thought she would never see her little friend again. If Cleopatra were still alive, she and Elizabeth would have gotten along well. They are both queens of the drama.

Jesus is now seven years old and has been attending the synagogue schools for his formal education. He is already a fluent reader, writer, and speaker of Aramaic and Greek. Now he is acquainting himself with the task of learning to read, write, and speak the Hebrew language. As always, he is eager to attend school and learn whatever he can.

Upon entering school this year as a result of a compulsory education law, each pupil chose a "birthday text," a sort of golden rule to guide them throughout their studies. Sometimes they recite this text at their graduation when they turn thirteen years old. The text Jesus chose from the Prophet Isaiah is an omen. He chose:

"The spirit of the Lord God is upon me,
for the Lord has anointed me;
he has sent me to bring good news to the meek,
to bind up the brokenhearted,
to proclaim liberty to the captives,
and to set the spiritual prisoners free."

Like all the other young boys, Jesus is growing in many other skills as well as his studies. All the mothers and young women of Nazareth talk with Jesus whenever he goes to draw water from the well which is one of the social centers of contact and gossip for the entire town. He is always entertaining them with his stories. Since we have more property with this house, we have purchased some goats which Jesus has learned to milk. He is currently learning to make cheese.

Today I had to take time to write about some more of Jesus' actions which are always amazing me. As I walked by the door, I saw Jesus and his new friends playing in the dirt. Alpheus and Rachel have come to help us move, so Matthew and James were also playing with them. A bird had built a nest in a tree in our front yard. A few days ago, four little birds hatched in the nest. I had watched the mother and father birds bring food for the babies. One of the baby bird's first attempts to fly turned into a disaster and the poor little bird landed a few feet from where the boys were playing. The little bird began chirping loudly and the boys quickly ran over to it. One of the boys reached down to pick it up and Jesus grabbed his arm and pulled him back. I watched as he and the boys discussed the matter.

After a few minutes, all the boys retreated and stood guard from a distance to protect the little bird. Before long, the mother bird flew down and gently nudged the tiny bird until he began to move. Once he moved, the mother guided him back to his nest. Instead of picking up the bird and playing with him as they wanted to do, Jesus persuaded his friends that the bird must not be touched or the mother would not come back. Later that day as the boys continued to play, the tiny bird again attempted to flee the nest. This time he had a successful flight. He flew above them for some time before Jesus lifted up his hand. The bird circled a few times and then perched on Jesus' shoulder. It pecked at his ear and cheek for a few seconds and then flew off again. Even the birds know he is special.

A few years ago, we let Jesus have a bird as a pet. He made a crude little cage from some of Joseph's scrap lumber. The first day, Jesus played with the bird in the cage. The next day he came to me in tears.

"Nothing my Father made should have to live their life in a cage. He made them to fly freely through the air. Why did I think the bird would be happy in a cage?" he asked through tear stained eyes.

After I assured him that he had done nothing wrong, he took the cage outside and lifted the bird to the wind. The little bird flew and circled Jesus for some time before he perched on his shoulder. Jesus smiled as the bird flew to his freedom.

Jesus is passionate about anyone mistreating any of the animals. The other day Jesus told our neighbor that his sheep needed to be in the shade on hot days. Everyone else doesn't appreciate his compassion as I do. Some think he is intruding and interfering, but he doesn't seem to care what people think as long as he is doing right. Jesus is a special son and I see it more every day. I am still worried that I may not know what he must do, but I am confident that God will show me the way.

We also have a family dog now. We let Jesus and James select one of the puppies from our neighbor's sheep dog. They decided to name him Blackie since he is mostly black with a few white spots. Blackie does not get out of Jesus' shadow. He is good about taking care of it. I think Jesus would go without food before he would let Blackie go hungry. They are true companions.

We celebrate happy events like everyone else. Jesus lost his first tooth a few days ago. He looked funny with the gap in his top teeth and a few days later he lost the other front one. Now he looks funny with a big gap in the front. James makes fun by calling him "toothless." Elizabeth feels sorry for him. She tried to make a clay mixture to fit in the gap to allow him to eat. Jesus sat patiently as she pushed and shoved trying to get the mixture to stick to his gum. It didn't work. I sometimes think he would stand on his head for hours if Elizabeth asked him to.

When Joseph has time, he often takes Jesus and James for walks. Since we have moved to this house, one of their favorite trips is to climb the high hill nearest our new house, from which they have a scenic view of all Galilee. To the northwest, on clear days, they can see the long ridge of

Mount Carmel running down to the sea. The boys enjoy hearing Joseph relate the story of Elijah, one of the first of the Hebrew prophets, who reproved Ahab and exposed the priests of Baal on that mountain.

Our new home offers such a beautiful view from all directions. To the north we can see the snowy peak of Mount Hermon rise majestically to the sky. Far to the east we can see the Jordan valley and the rocky hills of Moab. Also to the south and the east, when the sun shines upon their marble walls, we can view the Decapolis, with their amphitheaters and pretentious temples. To the west we can make out the sailing vessels on the distant Mediterranean.

From four directions we can observe the caravans as they wind their way in and out of Nazareth. To the south is the broad and fertile plain country stretching off toward Samaria where my friend, Christina, lives. I hope she and Silas and Alexa are doing well.

Jesus has a reverent respect for nature. He often takes James for a stroll through the countryside to study the various moods of the seasons.

Dear God Almighty, I see Your glorious splendor in the new environment in which we have moved. You have blessed me with such a wonderful family and now this bigger house with the breathtaking view which allows us to rejoice in Your great majesty. Everything about this move has been a part of Your divine plan. The purchase price is affordable, the setting is perfect, and the house is big enough for many more children. I know You have a reason for us to be here. I pray that I will recognize the signs You give me. You have always given us everything we've needed and then blessed us with a little more. Help us to be worthy of Your generosity.

Observe the month of Abib and celebrate the Passover of the Lord your God,
because in the month of Abib he brought you out of Egypt by night.
Deuteronomy 16:1

Jesus Asks Questions at the Passover Feast

It is unbelievable that I have not written an entry in over a year. With four children and the goats and sheep we now have, my life is busy. I am sad that my precious journal has remained under my cot most of this year. The only thing that has happened to our family since Joseph's birth is the death of poor Droopy. Last month we had to say goodbye to him. He saw us through a lot of tough times. I will never forget the day he smiled when we finally returned to our home in Nazareth. The children lost one of their playmates, Joseph lost a fellow worker and I lost a companion. To appease the children, we held a small ceremony for his burial. It is impossible to replace Droopy, but Joseph has already purchased another donkey which the children have named Ears because this one's ears stick straight up.

This week we are celebrating the Feast of the Passover. We always go to Jerusalem for this feast, but we also have a celebration at home as a time for friends and family to fellowship. This is the first year I've had the celebration at my house. We have always gone to mothers, but with my father's death, she did not feel like having everyone. The void left by the death of my father was more apparent than all the aunts, uncles, and cousins who were present. Everyone makes an effort to get together at this feast. Some years this is the only time I see Salome and her family. Elizabeth and Zechariah and John also came. When I saw them on John's birthday, I thought they would never be able to make this trip again, but they were determined to attend at least one more year to allow John and Jesus more time together. Elizabeth has aged considerably since I last saw her. I fear I will soon hear some bad news concerning her health.

Our families observe Passover for seven days. On the first day we observe the Passover meal or the Seder. Elizabeth helped me set the table for the celebration. Each setting has the four glasses of wine as well as a plate, cutlery, and napkin. We set a fifth glass of wine for Elijah. Several candles are placed on the table and the seating labels are placed. Servings of unleavened bread, vegetables, and vinegar and representative bottles of warm red wine are all in place on the table.

I am especially glad I could have it this year, since Jesus claimed the honor of asking the four questions. Usually it would have taken some practice for the questions, but after Jesus and I went over it once, he knew it all by heart. I sometimes feel he has seen all this before or took a part in it. It is really amazing, the details he knows. The reasons we celebrate Passover are known throughout the Jewish community, but when I tried to talk to Jesus about it, he ended up telling me about the death angel passing over the doors that had the drops of blood on them. I think he saw it happen. He told his siblings about the Israelites being held captive by the Egyptians, about Moses and the nine plagues before this tenth one. He knew of the turmoil that existed during the time as everyone wailed over the loss of their firstborn child. What a terrible thing. I wonder how much a part of all of this Jesus has been. I gave birth to him, but could he have been here before in some other form? What kind of relationship did he have with his heavenly father before he came to earth? What will be the role of a Messiah while he is on earth? I am still looking for that answer.

To begin the celebration, Joseph took one of the pieces of unleavened bread or matzah and broke it in half. He then wrapped half of it in a napkin and hid it in the house for the children to find at the end of the celebration. This custom helps hold the attention of the children until the end of the Seder.

We all sat around the table as the celebration continued with Jesus asking the four questions, which Joseph proudly answered. Jesus spoke humbly yet eloquently. The scene pleased everyone, including me. I knew he felt every word he spoke.

When he asked the question about dipping the herbs twice on this night instead of once, I thought he would cry. He felt the pain when he thought about dipping the bread into the herbs. I wonder how all of this is going to affect him. He seems to know much more than the rest of us. The entire celebration became an emotional experience for him.

When Joseph made the announcement to find the hidden bread, James quickly retrieved it. Then Joseph opened the door and we yelled for Elijah to come and save us. But like every other year, he didn't come. Jesus and John were strangely silent during that part of the ceremony. At the end of the ceremony, I saw them as they were discussing the meaning of the scripture that says Elijah will come back to save his people. What do they know about Elijah? If Jesus is the Messiah who is going to save us, what does this mean for those who are still expecting Elijah?

Do Jesus and John know what their relationship will be? Do they know how unique their births were and the bond that they share? Should I tell Jesus, or does he already know? I need to have a talk with him now that he is old enough to understand.

After the ceremony, everyone left except Zechariah, Elizabeth and John who are going to spend the night with us. We will travel back to Jerusalem with them. Elizabeth and I talked into the early morning. She still knows that Jesus will have his kingdom. Like me, she thought it would have already happened, but she has not given up hope that he will be that Messiah as promised by Gabriel. John, she knows, will be the voice in the wilderness, as spoken of by the prophet Isaiah. He will prepare the way for Jesus. I have faith, but Elizabeth has much more. Around her, my faith seems small and insignificant. My heartfelt desire is to understand as she does.

Dear God, as Your servant, I am here to do as You plan. Thank You for the wonderful experiences I have had nurturing Your son. Continue to show me the things You want me to do and help me know when the time is right for You to reclaim him. Thank You, also, for delivering the Israelites from the bondage of slavery. Where would we be if not for Your remarkable deliverance?

A Teacher Comes to Observe Jesus at Eight Years Old

This has been an interesting year for Jesus. At school he is a diligent pupil and among the top of his class. Because of this distinction, he is excused from attendance one week out of each month. That week he sometimes spends either with Joseph's fisherman brother on the shores of the Sea of Galilee near Magdala or on the farm of my brother, Judas, a half-day journey south of Nazareth. The last time Jesus stayed with Judas, he helped in the harvesting of the grain. Jesus is learning the skills of the fishermen and the farmers. Learning in the school is necessary, but nothing can compare to the experience he receives while performing a task with his own hands.

Although I am unduly anxious about his health and safety, I have gradually become reconciled to these trips away from home. Jesus' uncles and aunts are all fond of him, and usually compete among themselves to secure his company for these monthly visits throughout the year.

Jesus has also met a teacher of mathematics from Damascus who is teaching him some new techniques of numbers. He spends much time on mathematics, developing a keen sense of numbers which will help with the designs of the carpentry business. He works with James a lot to teach him the things he has learned.

This year Jesus made arrangements to exchange dairy products for lessons on the harp. Like the great King David, Jesus has an unusual liking for everything musical. When Jesus plays his harp, I can picture David sitting in his great mansion strumming those strings to create his beautiful Psalms. Jesus has tried without much success to promote an interest in music among his youthful friends. The boys are not nearly as interested in the music as Jesus.

Jesus continues to make enviable progress at school, but Joseph and I have not had the liberty to enjoy this advancement. He persists in asking many upsetting questions of the teachers. Questions such as why are there a dry season and a rainy season in Palestine or why is there a great difference between the temperature of Nazareth and the Jordan valley. He simply never ceases to ask such clever but confusing questions. His teachers have asked us repeatedly to talk to him. We can only shake our heads because we have tried.

In February, one of the teachers in a Jerusalem academy of the rabbis came to Nazareth to observe Jesus. Zechariah had instigated this visit after the teacher had visited John. The teacher at first seemed somewhat shocked by Jesus' frankness and unconventional manner of relating himself to things religious. Thinking that the remoteness of our home from the centers of Hebrew learning and culture was stifling Jesus' ability to receive a thorough education, the teacher advised Joseph and me to allow him to take Jesus back to Jerusalem. There he could have the advantages of education and training at the center of Jewish culture. I must admit that I could have been persuaded to consent since I know Jesus is to become the Messiah. However, Joseph, in his usual wisdom, hesitated. He was equally persuaded that Jesus needed to grow up to become a man of destiny, but what that destiny would prove to be he was uncertain. Joseph never really doubted that his son came to fulfill some great mission on earth, but since God had chosen us instead of a more cultured family, Joseph thought it would be best to teach Jesus at home. The more Joseph thought about the teacher's advice, the more he questioned the wisdom of the proposed stay in Jerusalem.

Not willing to give up easily, the teacher requested permission to lay the whole matter before Jesus. Jesus listened attentively as the teacher explained his offer. Then Jesus talked with me and Joseph. I thought my heart would break when he asked if we wanted him to leave home and go to Jerusalem. Joseph assured him that we have no intentions of making him go with the teacher unless he so desires.

I heard Jesus talking to his favorite playmate and his father, Jacob, the stone mason. "What?" Jacob asked. "Why would anyone think you could learn more in a rabbi school than you could living with this great school we are a part of everyday. You might become more knowledgeable, but you will *not* be more educated."

"I was thinking the same thing," Jesus said with a perceptive smile. I watched as Jesus went to sit under the shade and kneel in prayer. He needed to ask the greatest authority.

A few days later, Jesus asked to speak to the rabbi and Joseph and me. The four of us sat at our table as Jesus told us that he did not want to assume the responsibility of the decision since such a big difference of opinion existed among us and the teacher. He asked his heavenly Father for advice. "I'm not certain about His answer," Jesus said rubbing his chin, "but I feel I would like to remain at home with Mother and Father."

"I believe those who love me so much should be able to do more for me and guide me than strangers who want to view my body and observe my mine but hardly know me," Jesus said smiling at Joseph and me.

Joseph and I breathed a sigh of relief and the teacher thanked us and went his way, back to Jerusalem. Thankfully, we laid the subject of Jesus' going away from home to rest forever.

My dear Lord, You have blessed me with a child who possesses wisdom far beyond his years. I thank You for allowing him to stay close to home. Although my first instinct was to allow him to learn more from the teachers in Jerusalem, You showed Jesus that his life at home is far better suited to prepare him for the things he needs to know. I pray Father that we are worthy of Your approval. May we continue to teach him as You would have him learn in order to grow in mind and stature.

Mary Receives Word of Elizabeth's Death

Sadness covered my face as I blew two years of dust from my journal as I pulled it from beneath my bed tonight. There are many things I must record, but I am too embarrassed to even untie the ribbon that holds this precious document together. If I keep it closed, will no one know it has been that long? Reluctantly, I decided I must open it.

I received sad news from a messenger today. Elizabeth has gone to live with her Lord. We can no longer compare notes of our sons or contemplate what our futures may hold. I have chosen to honor her memory with a verse of Psalms.

Elizabeth

> Elizabeth, my dear friend,
>   I must tell you good-bye.
> God called you
>   And you willingly answered.
>
> I want to help with your son,
>   but I could never fill your shoes.
> I remember your words
>   spoken with gentleness wrapped in wisdom.
>
> Your heart loved your Lord.
> Your soul was destined even before
>   the angel answered your forgotten prayer.
> My soul grieves for another loved one gone.

Therefore…let us run with perseverance the race marked out for us.
Hebrews 12:1

Jesus Runs a Race

Today I was busy preparing a meal because my dear Joseph had graciously invited some travelers to stop and rest and take refreshment with us. This happens quite often. If Joseph has to go anywhere to check on a job, he usually comes back with some weary travelers. I almost complained once until he reminded me how grateful we were for the family that had gave us some rest on our way to Bethlehem. Joseph nearly gave up that day and I know I would have if a compassionate man had not taken us into his house and given us a good meal. The few hours rest from riding Droopy, restored my body in a way that I have not forgotten. For that reason, I graciously invite all the travelers into our home.

Today a man and his wife and ten year old son, Gamaliel, joined us. They were moving from Damascus to Jerusalem for Gamaliel to be taught by the teachers in a Jerusalem academy of the rabbis. It appears they received the same visit we received earlier this year. After they ate and rested for a few hours, they continued their travels. Everyone we have served has been appreciative. Our children enjoy meeting the new people and love to hear their stories. I know God would want me to help them and I am always spiritually revived after they leave. Each one promises to stop again if they are ever passing through. We have made many new friends this way. But now I must take some time to write about another incident.

My children and all the neighbors' children were outside playing. Even the young visitor Gamaliel stood at the edge of the group watching as the boys raced around trying to catch each other. I love to watch how fast Jesus can run. Joseph and I have often commented that we believe he could outrun a rabbit if he needed to, but he has never wanted to compete in any of the races. He is *not* a competitive child. Today a new boy in the group whose family had moved here from Egypt (I know what a hard trip that is) wanted to race. The boy bragged about how fast he could run and how he had been the champion runner in his old hometown. All the other children were listening and James blurted out, "Bet you can't beat my brother, Jesus. He's the fastest!"

The entire group of neighborhood kids joined in as Jesus quietly tried to slip away to talk to the shy new boy standing at the edge of the crowd. Even Elizabeth and the other girls stopped playing with their dolls long enough to listen to the dialogue. James kept yelling at Jesus to come on and race. Secretly, I had grown tired of listening to the yelling and also wanted Jesus to try and win—only one time. Finally Jesus gave in to the pleading and the boys lined up. The new boy from Egypt scoffed at Jesus' lanky stature.

When James said "Go!" the boys took off like a streak of lightening. No doubt the new boy had some speed, but I knew Jesus could run faster. They were tied most of the way. I saw Jesus pull ahead a little bit as a look of panic swept across the new boy's face. Jesus, close enough to see it also, immediately slowed enough to let the boy cross the finish line one step ahead of him.

James became furious! He fussed at Jesus for giving up. Jesus only smiled and said, "I ran the only race I knew how."

The new boy came over and shook Jesus' hand and whispered, "Thanks".

All the other boys rushed up to congratulate the new boy and Jesus quietly wandered off alone. I watched him for awhile as he sat with Blackie at his side under the shade tree in our back yard. The little bird flew down and rested on his shoulder, just like the last time. Jesus smiled and said something. They sat there for a few minutes until the bird finally flew into the sky. I can't help but wonder if this is the same little bird Jesus saved from all the boys, or if it is really a bird at all.

After a few minutes, the visitor, Gamaliel, went over to sit beside Jesus and they talked for the longest time. Jesus has always been able to make friends easily. I'm sure if they meet again they will recognize each other.

Jesus could have won that race if he really wanted to win, but making a friend is more important to him than the glory. It is times like this I remember who Jesus really is. In everyday happenings, I forget and consider him another one of the children, but every once in a while he does something out of the ordinary to remind me how exceptional he is.

I wish I knew more about what is going to happen. The brief talks I have had with Jesus trying to explain about his birth have been surprisingly easy. I dreaded telling him for fear of his reaction, but as usual, my worries were unfounded. He looked at me sincerely and simply said, "I love you, Mother. I fear what my destiny may cause you. You should not worry, for you must know that when I do some things, I am going about my Father's business. Always know, no matter what, that I love you with a special part of my heart."

He gave me a big hug and walked away. I think he knows and understands even at this young age.

Dear God, please help me be as patient as Your son. Help me to understand what he must do. Sometimes I try to forget, but when I stop to think about it, I am overwhelmed with awe and bewilderment of what our future may hold. I only know our future abides in Your unchanging plan.

Jesus' Twelfth Birthday

We celebrated a big birthday for Jesus today. Young Jewish boys are considered to reach manhood at thirteen, but they begin to assume more responsibility at twelve. This year Jesus said the prayer of thanks to God at his birthday. It's hard to believe Jesus has been here for twelve years. At first, I watched him with a protective eye. After all, he is God's son and great things must come from him. There have been younger boys than Jesus who have become king. Joash became a king at only four years old. I still don't know what to expect, but I do think it will happen soon.

After the other children were born, Jesus' unique birth became lost in the hustle and bustle of living and dealing with a growing family. At first, I had a concern about having other children. I thought maybe all my attention should have been focused on Jesus, and questioned if I could treat other children fairly. Joseph convinced me that if God gave his son to us, he expected us to raise him like we would our own child and that means having brothers and sisters. Now after twelve years and four kids, Jesus is as normal as any of his siblings.

While I wait for something to happen, Jesus continues to grow strong in stature and in mind. My limited knowledge has been exhausted for teaching the children, but they want much more. Like all the other children, the boys have gone to the synagogue for their required studies, but they have advanced beyond that. I teach Elizabeth at home. She is as smart as the boys and enjoys learning the writing skills.

It is important for Jesus to gain as much knowledge as possible since he is being prepared for his kingdom. There is no end to what he is willing to learn. He is not only fluent in Aramaic, but also knows much Greek and even Hebrew. The stories of the Greek Gods do not amuse him. He enjoys learning about the prophets and memorizing the laws of Moses.

Although Jesus might have enjoyed a better opportunity for schooling had he gone with the teacher to Jerusalem, he could not have had such a splendid environment for working out his own life problems. Here at home, he enjoys the advantage of constantly contacting with men and women of all classes hailing from different parts of the civilized world.

Had he left, his education would have been directed by Jews and along exclusively Jewish lines. I feel Jesus did correctly interpret his Father's guidance. At Nazareth he is securing an education and receiving training which will give him a better and more balanced idea of other cultures. This should be helpful when he receives his kingdom.

Jesus is also a good worker for Joseph. At twelve he will begin taking a major role in the business. He will now go with Joseph when he works outside his shop. Joseph is amazed with his mathematical ability when he asks him to figure the arches of the houses he builds. At twelve, he is much quicker with numbers than Joseph. He also has a keen artistic eye. We went to examine the last house as Joseph worked on it and Jesus quickly saw that the arc of the angle did not appear correct. His suggestion saved Joseph from making a big mistake in the final details.

As good as he is in the carpentry business, his heart is in his music. He loves to hum the Psalms of the great King David as he works. His voice, unlike mine, sounds like the melodious nightingales. Everyone has greatly enjoyed Jesus' extraordinary interpretations of the Psalms on his harp. It is hard for me to think that someone as gentle and soft spirited as he is, will ever become that king as the angel promised. I still sometimes think I had a dream until I remember the details of his miraculous birth. Joseph never mentions anything, but I think he may be more anxious than I am for this kingdom to appear. However, we will be patient because no matter how much we doubt at times, we both know who Jesus really is and know that our only job at this time is to raise him as best we can.

John and Zechariah came to visit for the first time since Elizabeth's death. It is strange watching John and Jesus together without Elizabeth here to compare notes. Sorrow for her company floods my soul. I will have to speak to her spirit and listen for her answer. My Elizabeth cried when she realized her namesake was not going to be with them.

John and Jesus are so different and yet so alike. Their love for memorizing the scriptures and their comprehension of what they memorize is beyond anything I have ever witnessed. Zechariah told how John goes to the synagogue with him and amazes everyone with his knowledge and wisdom. He has already made a few of the Pharisees and Sadducees angry when he corrects them and tells them what the laws really say. He knows the true scripture like Jesus. I fear his outspoken personality will someday get him in trouble.

Dear God, I pray You will watch carefully over these two boys. They are destined for whatever You ask them to do. Please give them the strength they need to complete the tasks You must ask of them. Give us the wisdom to stay out of their way and let them complete the tasks You have already planned for them.

When he was twelve years old, they went up to the Feast, according to
the custom… When they did not find him, they went back to Jerusalem.
After three days they found him in the temple courts, sitting among
the teachers, listening to them and asking them questions.
Luke 2: 41-52

Jesus at the Temple

What a terrible time this has been. Our trip to the temple in Jerusalem to observe Passover turned disastrous, but also revealing. We felt compelled to make the trip this year since Jesus will soon graduate from one of the schools of the synagogue of Nazareth. He will be presented to us by the rulers as an educated "son of the commandment"—henceforth a responsible citizen of the commonwealth of Israel, all of which requires his attendance at the Passover.

We made the long, tiring trip without incident. With four children, Blackie, and another child on the way, Joseph and I had our hands full. Three of the families in our party were invited to stay in the house of a friend, Simon, in Bethany. There we observed the Passover meal with him and his family. Lazarus, Simon's son, took Jesus, James and Blackie throughout Bethany observing the shops and workers. Mary and Martha, Simon's daughters, entertained Elizabeth and Joseph during the day. Jesus and Lazarus were constant companions from the minute we arrived at their house until we left to go to Jerusalem to meet the rest of our caravan. I think Jesus will want to spend many Passover feasts in the house of his new friend and his family who were very gracious hosts.

Others families from our caravan met us at the temple. We completed the observance and began the trip home. I assumed Jesus had gone to travel with some of his friends or cousins to tell them of his adventures in Bethany. I wasn't worried because he would show up in time to eat, like he always does. At mealtime he still had not arrived, but I didn't get too concerned because the children often eat with the family who has the best and most food. Worry surfaced as darkness began to blanket the night sky. I had struggled with mild nausea most of the day. My body was saying, "Please rest" but my mind was wide awake waiting for Jesus to return.

When Joseph came and said he couldn't find Jesus, I nearly panicked.

We had lost Jesus—the son God had entrusted to our care. I have an abundant amount of faith that God will take care of everything, but like all mothers, when it comes to your child, I sometimes overlook the obvious. Jesus is a good boy who always does what we ask and never causes us any worry. Today my level of worry rose to the sky. The roads are not safe and I knew something bad had happened for Jesus not to come to our site. I repeatedly apologized to God for losing His precious son. Prayers for his safety poured from my soul.

We were about midway of the caravan. Joseph had to go all the way to the beginning to make sure he had not traveled ahead of us. James and Elizabeth ran to the back. I stayed at our site with Joseph in case Jesus returned. No one could remember seeing Jesus since we left the city. The weariness of the day swept over me as the sky began to sway. James and Elizabeth gently helped me sit down. Knowing that I could not travel any further without rest, Joseph decided we needed a good night's sleep to prepare for a trip back to the city early tomorrow morning. James wanted to start out that night with Joseph while I took the other children home, but my instinct told me that Joseph and I must go. Without the light of a bright star to guide us, it would have been impossible to travel at night. Salome agreed to take James, Elizabeth and Joseph back to Nazareth and wait until we returned with Jesus. The children love spending time with their aunt, and I knew they would be well cared for. I also knew James and Elizabeth would worry until we returned. At five, Joseph would miss us the most, but would worry the least.

My mind wandered back to the night of Jesus' birth and I immediately knew that God would keep His son safe. He did not send him to earth to be lost on a trip to Jerusalem. I knew of Jesus' safety, but I also knew we needed to find him. The rest my body longed for did not come that night. All the children were restless and worried except James. He kept telling us Jesus knew how to take care of himself and he would catch up with us. We decided not to wait and find out. At the first crack of dawn, Joseph and I started our weary trip. James, Elizabeth and Joseph bravely waved good-bye as Salome's arms encircled them.

On the long, hot trip we had to be careful of animals and thieves since there were only the two of us, but with only two we were able to travel much faster. We checked with every other caravan we met, but to no avail. He was not to be found.

When we returned to Jerusalem, we were at a loss as to where to start. Hustle and bustle of the overcrowded streets hindered our search. The guidance I desperately needed did not come. Why did God want us to roam aimlessly for what seemed an eternity? Even though I felt certain Jesus was safe, weariness flooded my being. Maybe God intended to punish us for not keeping a closer watch on His son. Although I knew in the back of my mind that God's plan guided our path, fear of something bad happening to His son crept into my thoughts. Without a miracle, he could not have survived by himself for this length of time. Caught up in my worry, I forgot he is never alone.

When we arrived at the temple on the third day, a huge crowd had gathered causing a great commotion in the courtyard. Joseph and I pushed our way through the crowd still searching for Jesus. A familiar gentle voice floated over the crowd causing my heart to leap for joy. I wanted to rush to him and cover him with hugs and kisses before I scolded him for not staying with us. Joseph grabbed my hand and we both stopped, frozen in our tracks. Jesus was sitting in the center of the crowd with all the teachers. They were discussing the affairs of the day and the laws of ancient times. We listened, as Jesus held his own with the scholars. Like the rest of the crowd, we stood and watched for some time. His knowledge of the old laws of the scriptures astounded everyone. The scholars were being forced to think outside their regular teachings with his ability to comprehend and interpret what had been written many years ago.

Interrupting that discussion was out of the question. Especially since the urgency of our search had disappeared. We were no longer concerned for his safety, and starting back at this time of the day would have been impossible.

Joseph and I marveled at the scene. Joseph started to step forward, but this time I grabbed his arm. Something told me that he should not be interrupted. A higher power had initiated this dialogue that Jesus needed to finish. I couldn't recall any specific prophecies that foretold this particular event, but my heart told me he needed to continue.

When they finally took a break, I made my way to him and asked what he was doing. His answer should have shocked me, but it didn't. He looked me straight in the eyes and respectfully asked, "Mother, why were you searching for me? Don't you know that I must be about my Father's business?"

I returned to Joseph and we both listened with the rest of the crowd as he continued to awe everyone with his amazing ability to interject his knowledge and comprehension of the scriptures into the intense discussions.

When they finally finished late that evening, Jesus came to us and calmly said "I am ready to go home. Let's go." I don't know why God allowed this incident to happen, but I do know that God's son already knows what he must and must not do. Joseph and I are obligated to remember that God's will must come first in our lives. It doesn't look like we will have much say in the matter. God has a plan and we are a small part of it.

I know that I cannot be overbearing and must give Jesus the time and space he needs to be about his Father's business. I can only marvel and cherish these memories in a special place in my heart until I can record them as accurately as possible for the world to know. Thankfully, God has always provided the material and time for me to do this. Like tonight, we were invited to stay in one of the teacher's house. Joseph and Jesus took a cot to the roof to sleep, but I knew I would not be able to sleep in this strange environment. Before our host reclined I asked if I could use some of his papyrus. With a curious look, he told me to help myself. Everyone else is asleep as I record this amazing event.

Usually, I try to think of Jesus as an average child. Only at times like today I am reminded that he is truly God's son. I expect any day to discover the meaning of the angel's promise, but things go along smoothly and it seems his kingdom may be a long time away. After the event today, I again think it may be around the corner. God is preparing him for something big. He is preparing me too, I am afraid. Jesus' wisdom, compassion and comprehension at this young age far exceed most of the older experienced men around, including the Pharisees and Sadducees in the temple. I again feel Simeon's sword piercing my heart.

Dear God, help me discover the truth and the way. Our son is growing strong willed and mature in his thinking. I must let You have Your way, but it is hard to give him up. He is still my flesh and blood. My heart will always have a special place for him. I am excited about this kingdom he will inherit, but I fear that my heart may suffer much before he obtains it. Give me strength and courage to bear whatever You ask of me.

Deborah is Born Prematurely

Today my heart is heavy with a deep sadness. A few months after Joseph and I conceived this child, we had to go to Jerusalem for the Passover. There we lost Jesus. Instead of realizing the incident was a part of God's plan, I chose to worry and fret for many days. I fear all that stress may have somehow harmed my baby. My mother always said to keep a strong healthy mind when with a child.

As I lay in bed drained from this experience, I must write while everything is fresh in my mind. I gave birth today to a precious baby girl. I only carried her a few months, but I could still tell she was a little girl. The sharp pains came quickly followed by a surge of bleeding. In a short time my baby, tiny and still was born. We didn't even need to summon the midwife. Unable to bear this heartache again, I am definitely not having any more children.

Deborah fit in the palm of my hand. No one wanted me to hold her, but I needed to see God's precious child. I wrapped her in some swaddling cloths and cuddled her like I have all the rest of my babies. The young soul didn't exist anymore. She had already gone to be with her heavenly Father. The pain tears through my heart, but I know God will take good care of her. He gave me His son and He has chosen to take my precious little daughter.

Jesus stood by my side and for an instant my eyes pleaded with him. After I saw her, I knew he did all he could. In my heart I know that if God had instructed him, Jesus could have given her life. Jesus looked at me with tears in his eyes and shook his head. I understood and immediately felt at peace.

As they took her to prepare her for burial, everyone left me alone to get some much needed rest. Jesus came back into my room and walked over and took my hand and kissed me on the forehead. "Dear mother," he said with tear-filled eyes. "I wanted to, but I couldn't. Her living was not a part of Father's plan. He has already taken her lovely soul to be with him. She will never suffer a minute's pain. She is the lucky one. We must prepare you for other things that will happen. Birth is a wonderful thing, but death is also. We must learn to let go when one is called by my Father. When He is ready, He will take all of us. Sad as it may be, we must learn to rejoice for the soul that has gone to heaven to live in that beautiful mansion. It is truly beautiful, Mother."

He turned and left me staring. What is he telling me? Is heaven the mansion I have been looking for all these years? Will that be his ultimate kingdom? Will we never see that mansion—the throne of David? He is warning me that I must start preparing my mind for whatever is going to happen to him. Why does he always seem contented when he speaks about death and heaven? "It is beautiful," he said. Has he been there? Has he walked those streets paved with gold? Is this something I will experience with him?

Dear God, You must help me prepare for what Jesus is telling me. I look at my life a little differently now. I have patiently waited many years for that mansion mentioned by the angel. "The kingdom of David," he said. Is that heaven? Did You send Jesus to earth until he grew up enough to join You? Will You take him from me to go to heaven? If that is so, what is his purpose on this earth? How I wish I had some answers. But I pray that I will never again have to endure the pain I have suffered with this birth. If You must take him, please do it quickly and quietly. I could not stand to see him suffer. I must go now and prepare to bury my precious little Deborah. Please take good care of her. She is also special. Thank You for all the wonderful children You have graciously given me to love.

And Jesus grew in wisdom and stature, and in favor with God and men.
Luke 2:52

Jesus' Thirteenth Birthday

Joseph and I are preparing for a big year for Jesus. As he turned thirteen today, he automatically became obligated by God's commandments as interpreted by Moses. Prior to this birthday, Joseph and I were responsible for his obedience to Jewish law and traditions. He is now eligible to count in a prayer quorum, lead prayer services and testify before a religious court. Jesus can now be asked to participate in the Sabbath service as an adult. I feel he will often be asked to read the Hebrew Scriptures to the faithful assembled in the synagogue.

Last week as Jesus and I were walking to get water, we started talking about how some of the Jews consider themselves much higher than the gentiles. I wanted to tell him about Christina, the young girl I met in Samaria when I was going to visit Elizabeth, but he doesn't know that I left home for a few months. I still remember how the family that brought me back from Elizabeth's scorned all the gentiles we met along the road. As if reading my mind, Jesus surprised me by saying, "Everyone should love their neighbors."

"It is easy to love your neighbors," I replied.

His mouth turned up in a simple smile as he said, "Everyone is your neighbor, Mother. Even the gentiles who pass through here on the caravans are your neighbors in your heavenly Father's eyes. It is the meek who will inherit the earth. Those who are merciful will be shown mercy in return. And the pure in heart are the ones God will allow in heaven. There is no time for hatred of our brothers. Mother, don't people realize everyone is a child of my Father? How can He love someone whose heart is filled with hatred for one of His children? How would you feel toward someone who openly scorned one of your children?"

"They would *not* be welcome in my house," I said as he laughed.

James and Elizabeth joined us and we had to stop. I adore having these conversations with him. He asks such thought-provoking questions that make sense. Why *do* we disrespect the Gentiles? They are God's people, too. I can see that Jesus will not be well received by the Jewish leaders. I fear his thinking may cause him some problems.

When I see Jesus conversing with the caravan travelers and conductors, I understand why God did not guide him to go to the synagogue in Jerusalem to study with the teachers. In Nazareth Jesus can mingle freely with the caravans as they tarry near the spring for rest and nourishment. In Galilee the Jews mingle more freely with the gentiles than is the practice in Judea. And of all the cities of Galilee, Nazareth places the least restrictions based on the fears of contamination as a result of contact with the gentiles. These conditions often give rise to the common saying in Jerusalem, "Can any good thing come out of Nazareth?" This really concerns me when I think that Jesus must convince others that he is Messiah, the son of God, when they know he comes from Nazareth.

I have mixed feelings about Jesus reaching this birthday. If he is considered an adult, will his heavenly Father think it is time for him to receive his kingdom? Jesus is mature for his age, but I still can't vision him being a ruler over a kingdom. Although he would do a much better job than most.

Dear God, You have blessed us with Your son for thirteen years. As I watch him become a man, I wonder how much longer I will have him. He grows daily in his love for You as well as his love for Your word. Help us to know what You want of him and guide us in that direction.

He went to Nazareth, where he had been brought up, and on the Sabbath day
he went into the synagogue, as was his custom. And he stood up to read.
Luke 4:16

Jesus Reads in the Synagogue

I haven't written about any of our ceremonies in the synagogue because they are usually the same every Sabbath. Today the service was different. This morning the sun peeked over the mountaintop as we walked up the rise to the synagogue. We have done this nearly every Sabbath since Joseph and I have been in Nazareth. Elizabeth and I took our seats in the benches reserved for the women while Joseph and the boys took seats in their reserved area. We are not allowed to worship together. Women can only listen and not participate. In front of the chest containing the scrolls of the Law and the Prophets, the religious leaders sat in their elaborate chairs.

With the required ten males present for the public worship, a rabbi began the service with the usual recitation of the Shema, "Hear, O Israel: Jehovah our God is one Jehovah: and thou shall love Jehovah thy God with all thy heart, and with all thy soul, and with all thy might". The "Blessed" sentences of praise to God accompanied this recitation.

Following the Shema the usual ritual prayer was said, concluding with an opportunity for individual silent prayer on the part of the members.

This is when the order of service changed a bit. The rabbi in charge of the service took the scroll of Isaiah from the chest, opened it to a scripture and handed it to Jesus and asked him if he would like to read today. Joseph beamed with pride as Jesus eagerly jumped up, walked up to the platform with the reading desk and opened the scrolls of Isaiah to a different scripture than what the rabbi had given him. I couldn't remember all the scripture he read, but I do remember Zechariah reading this passage when I stayed with him and Elizabeth. He read this often to encourage me. How did Jesus know to choose this particular scripture? He read:

A voice of one calling:
"In the desert prepare
The way for the Lord;
make straight in the wilderness
a highway for our God.
Every valley shall be raised up,
every mountain and hill made low;
the rough ground shall become level,
the rugged places a plain.
And the glory of the Lord will be revealed,
and all mankind together will see it.
For the mouth of the Lord has spoken."

Jesus continued reading the prophet's words as the congregation listened. Usually after sitting for some time, everyone begins squirming in their seats, anxious for the rabbi to finish. Today was different. Jesus held everyone's attention for some time. He spoke Isaiah's words with such authority. Did he help write this scripture? He knew exactly where to put the emphasis. I heard groans of disappointment when he finally rolled up the scrolls and returned them to the rabbi.

Jesus then explained the scripture he read. He said that God had sent someone to prepare a way for Messiah. He didn't say God was going to send, but that He had sent. As he explained more, my mind drifted to the Passover celebration when he and John did not call for Elijah. They know. At thirteen, they know who they really are. How difficult can this be for them—to know, but not be able to reveal their secret to anyone? Jesus' interpretation amazed the men, even Joseph. The rabbi then closed the service with a blessing.

We walked back down the rise to our house where Jesus went out to the tree and sat for awhile. I looked out once and the bird was perched on his shoulder. I know that bird is a sign from his heavenly Father. Was God as impressed with His son today as I was?

James asked why Jesus was asked to read today. I told him Jesus had passed the age of responsibility and would probably read much more. "I don't want to do that," I heard James mumble as he walked outside.

Elizabeth commented on how beautiful the service was this morning. The rest of his siblings didn't question the incident. They are so used to Jesus reading to them that they didn't think there was anything extraordinary about him reading for the rabbi. It really wasn't unusual. Many boys read in the synagogue after they turn thirteen, but I've never heard anyone read with such conviction. The reading was peaceful but authoritative. The rabbi didn't pick the particular scripture for Jesus. He knew exactly what he wanted to read. I know God is preparing His son for something great. Today reminds me that there really is something going on. Like everyone else, I will just have to wait and hope.

Dear God, thank You for allowing us to hear Your son today. We will have lots of visitors tomorrow. People will want to know where Jesus received his remarkable skill of understanding the scriptures. I will tell them his Father taught him. That would be the truth, only they will doubt that Joseph is capable of such teaching. Although Joseph is knowledgeable of the scriptures of Isaiah, he does not possess the ability to interpret as Jesus does. Give me the wisdom to face their questions with the truth.

Isn't this the carpenter's son? Isn't his mother's name Mary,
and aren't his brothers James, Joseph, Simon and Judas?
Matthew 12:46-47; 13:55-56; Mark 3:31-32; Luke 8:19-20

Simon is Born and Jesus Heals James' Hand

My writings have been few and far between these last few years. When I unpacked the parchment tonight, I was ashamed to see it has been over a year since my last entry. I want to keep a better record, but life is so full!

After the premature birth of Deborah, I vowed to never have another baby. With Joseph's work and a house full of children, our times together are not as often as we would hope. When we do find a chance to totally enjoy each other as husband and wife, the desire God gave us is as strong today as the first time we experienced that wonderful union in our makeshift house in the cave. Ashamedly, we are sometimes a little careless. I gave birth to baby Simon a week ago.

Things are busy with another baby in the house. I sincerely hope this is my last child. Joseph and I are not getting any younger and each child saps more energy from both of us. If Jesus didn't help care for his brothers and Elizabeth didn't take over the housework, we could not make it. As a young girl, I remember Cousin Elizabeth coming to stay with Mother and Father for a few days. She would pamper me by brushing my hair and fixing it fancy with pins and ornaments. Those memories are dear to me. My Elizabeth has the same adoring heart toward her siblings. She can care for them as well as I can. Even young Joseph tries to comfort baby Simon when he cries. God has blessed me with a house full of caring children.

We named him Simon after Joseph's little brother. All our children love their Uncle Simon. Since he has been married for a few years without being blessed with any children, he is happy doting on ours. Now that he has moved closer, we get to see him much more than we used to. He is also a righteous and devout man who will make an excellent namesake for our new son.

Simon is as healthy a baby as the rest have been except Deborah. It is sometimes difficult for me to understand how my body can produce such a healthy child one time and such an unhealthy one the next. Joseph smiled and said the easy birth resulted from all the practice I have had. I don't think he would care if we had a dozen children. He would love them all equally.

Fortunately Jesus and Elizabeth want to help. If I had to depend on James, I would be in trouble. He does not like to do anything around the house, but he loves to hunt and fish. I can always count on him to bring meat and fish for our supper.

I had to take time to jot down the miraculous event I witnessed today. The angel told me Jesus is to be a king but I am not sure what that means. Even King David and Solomon in all their glory did not possess the miraculous healing powers that I witnessed today.

While nursing baby Simon, I sat at the window watching Jesus and James playing outside. They are both as agile as little monkeys. There is a big tree beyond our house where James and Jesus are building a small house out of scrap material from Joseph's shop for their brothers and sisters to play in. It sets about ten feet off the ground in a fork of the tree. They were resting on the floor of the house when a little bird landed on a branch beside them. James, being a brave young boy, stood on all fours and started inching toward the little bird. I held my breath as he quietly reached for the small bird and slipped off the branch. He landed on the ground with a horrible thump as Jesus scurried down the tree to him. With a sleeping baby in my lap, I struggled to get there.

As Jesus helped James stand up, I saw James' hand hanging loosely from his wrist. His piercing scream enforced my thought that it was broken and brought Joseph running from his shop. As Jesus touched James's hand, the crying stopped. James stared at Jesus in wonder, as Joseph joined them. "Ah, he's fine," Jesus said as he tousled his brother's hair. "Father, you can go back to work now."

Not being able to see the hand as I did, Joseph couldn't understand the reason for the scream. I could only stare in amazement as Jesus and his brother took off down the road laughing and racing. Joseph smiled and shook his head as he slowly walked back to his shop.

Since the incident at the temple, I have been telling Jesus more about his birth. I told him the story of a baby being conceived by the Holy Spirit. I almost told him word for word what the angel told me about a king being born. Earlier when I had told him about the angelic visit to Zechariah, he didn't even act surprised. He smiled when I told him how

Zechariah had questioned the angel and couldn't speak until he named the baby "John." I told him about Elizabeth's baby leaping in her womb when I went to visit her. He doesn't know why I went to visit. It would break his heart to think that Joseph had intended to quietly divorce me when he found out I was with child. It still bothers Joseph to think about it. That secret will always remain with me, Joseph, Alpheus and my journal. If it is ever known, Alpheus will have to be the one to tell it.

A few days ago I told Jesus more details of his birth. He looked up at me and asked if the story was true. I knew he wanted to ask more when I told him it was. Instead he went outside to be alone and sit under his favorite tree. I watched as the little bird came and rested on his shoulder again. I know this bird is a sign. Every time Jesus does something miraculous or needs to meditate, this little bird mysteriously appears from nowhere and rests on his shoulder. Jesus knelt in reverent prayer for some time. He knows he is that baby and that he and John have a special bond. At the temple, Jesus acted as if he knows who he really is, but I think he is a little young to fully understand what it all means. The miraculous power he possessed today has to make him wonder, as it does me, what is in store for him.

I pray that Joseph and I will be able to accept what is going to happen and that we recognize the signs God provides. Today the sign indicated that God is preparing him for great things. Joseph didn't see what happened to James' hand today. I will not tell him at this time because he already worries about what he knows must happen. He probably knows a little deeper than I do and understands the task that is ahead of Jesus. Joseph knows he has been entrusted to raise this son and he is determined to be the best father possible. He will worry more if he knows Jesus is already able to perform miracles as he did today. As usual, I will have to keep these things secretly in my heart, and in this journal, until the time comes to make them known.

Dear God, thank You for allowing Jesus to heal James's hand today. Jesus has mighty powers but I know he has nothing without You. Give me the understanding to know that what he does is all a part of Your glorious design. Help Joseph and me be the parents You want us to be. I pray that little Simon will be as big a blessing as all my other children.

A righteous man may have many troubles, but the Lord delivers him from them all; he protects all his bones, not one of them will be broken.
Psalms 34: 19-20
These things happened so that the scripture would be fulfilled: "Not one of his bones will be broken,"
John 19: 36

Jesus Suffers no Broken Bones

We returned from observing the Passover celebrations a few days ago. We enjoyed staying with Simon and his family again. He has invited us to stay every year. They have a big house with room for all of us especially since the boys go to the roof to sleep. Jesus and Lazarus are constantly together when we are there. They have undoubtedly examined every stone in that town. At first James wanted to tag along, but this time he and Joseph did some exploring on their own. We are so thankful that God has given us good friends and a place to stay when we go to Jerusalem.

Today as I sat at the door mending some of the holes in the boy's tunics, I witnessed a miraculous event. Strange but wonderful things often happen, but today Jesus truly performed another miracle. Jesus, at fourteen, is such a typical child that I often forget what the angel told me. Days like today refresh my memory.

The kids were playing in the street with some type of ball. Jesus ran with the ball as the other boys chased him. Someone fell in front of Jesus and he tripped over the boy. The kids behind Jesus fell on top of him in a big pile. My body cringed as I saw his leg bend completely back. I knew it had to be broken. There is no way a limb could bend like that and stay whole. I ran out to him as fast as I could. Suspecting Jesus would not be able to stand alone, I reached down to help. My heart waited anxiously for the piercing scream of pain. Instead he looked at me and jumped straight up. The boys had also seen his leg and were standing in wonder until Jesus quickly grabbed the ball and took off for the game to continue.

I went back to the house amazed. How could that have happened? His father saw it too. When I straightened up, Joseph stood beside me with a tear in his eye. He had expected the worst also. We looked at each other with a knowing glance and went back to our business. Jesus should have had a broken bone, but God chose not to let it happen. I looked out at the boys and the little bird circled above them. Jesus looked up and winked at it.

As soon as possible, I am going to go study some of the Psalms. I remember the mention of broken bones in one of them. Something about no bones shall be broken. If I read the scriptures closely enough, I can probably predict Jesus' whole life. Maybe I should ask him what is going to happen to him. He can probably give me a detailed description. Maybe he could tell me when that kingdom is going to arrive.

Jesus is becoming as much of a teacher as I am to his brothers and Elizabeth. They all listen intently when he speaks. He has such an authoritative, but soothing voice. He clearly demands their attention. I could sat and listen to him for hours when he is talking.

Jesus is now often asked to conduct the morning services in the synagogue. He is always ready to read the scripture, but if any distinguished visitor is present, they are asked to address the synagogue. Jesus is receiving a good sampling of different cultures from the many great thinkers who often speak.

Dear God, help me more fully understand what You have prepared for him. Give me the courage to accept and the wisdom to know what is happening. Help me better understand the words of the prophets and psalmists as they foretell Jesus' life. I pray that I will not worry when I read and understand what is to come. I also pray for this child I am carrying. I fear I may be getting too old to properly care for a little baby.

Isn't this the carpenter's son? Isn't his mother's name Mary,
and aren't his brothers James, Joseph, Simon and Judas?
Matthew 12:46-47; 13:55-56; Mark 3:31-32; Luke 8:19-20

Judas is Born

This has been a long nine months, but it is finally over. Judas arrived in all his glory a week ago. My body looked like an old wineskin ready to burst. I could hardly walk the entire last month. Again Jesus and Elizabeth came to my rescue by taking over the care of the little ones. It is very natural for Elizabeth, at eleven, to care for her siblings. She has a gentle spirit like her namesake. However, most boys at sixteen would not be as willing to help with the house work as Jesus does. God has truly blessed me with patient and caring children.

I am glad for this time to catch up with some of my writing. Jesus, James and Joseph are attending school in the synagogue. The teachers are constantly telling Joseph how they are also learning from Jesus' pointed questions. Sometimes one of the scholars comes here to discuss questions with Jesus. Many of the teachers often come by to play a game of senet with him. He could beat any of them anytime, but he usually thinks the wiser of it and allows them to win unless they make a stupid move. Then they will laugh and acknowledge what an easy game. I'm still teaching Elizabeth and Simon.

Of course Elizabeth enjoys dressing up in the fancy clothes Lydia gives her, more than she enjoys studying. Like my parents, I believe it is important for girls to have an education. I believe I would never have been chosen to raise God's son had I not been able to read and record these events for the world to see this part of Jesus' life.

Joseph is working nearly sixteen hours a day in his shop. Sometimes I think he is happier in his shop than he is in this noisy house. I know I would be. Not really, I love the hustle and bustle of all the children enjoying life to the fullest. Jesus and James help their Father considerably when they are not studying. They love being in the shop with him and he enjoys the help. He often comments on the level of detail work that Jesus can do. Everyone expects that Jesus will become a master craftsman someday. We both know that will not happen.

Mary, Martha and Lazarus have come to help for a few days. Martha is a blessing around the house. She and Elizabeth have become very close as they complete the necessary chores. If Martha insists, Mary helps also, but she prefers to spend time in the shop with Jesus and Lazarus. Those boys have become true friends. It is delightful watching the three of them laughing as they discuss the trials of the day. Mary often sits and watches the boys compete in a good-humored game of senet.

James and Joseph are old enough that they are not any trouble, and Simon is like their little shadow. I have birthed so many babies I could probably do it by myself, but it is really nice having a few days of rest to catch up on my writing. Although I love to write, by the time I get everything done at night, I'm so tired I don't have the energy. Now while the baby is asleep and the rest of the children are occupied, I am in my own little heaven preserving more memories.

This birth of the smallest of all my babies thus far has been the easiest of them all. The doctor says he is fine as long as he is able to nurse. Today he has nursed extremely well. Even though I love babies, I am not as young as I used to be and each addition adds much work. It would have been easier if this one had been a girl who could share a room with Elizabeth. All the boys share one room, which is not a problem since they delight in sleeping on the roof so Jesus can teach them about the wondrous heavens and stars in all their glory.

Our bigger house is starting to get a little crowded. Joseph says he will begin work on another room as soon as he finishes the current projects he is working on. I have heard that before and don't expect it to happen any time soon. No matter how tired Joseph is when he comes to the house, he always takes the time to tell the children a story. Sometimes he barely makes it to the end before he falls asleep.

This baby was named after my older brother. I think my brother was disappointed when we named our last son after Joseph's brother. Judas is a farmer by trade, but he spends a lot of time in the synagogue discussing things with the priests and teachers. He asked me the other day if I thought the Messiah spoken about in Isaiah would be born during our lifetime. I wanted to tell him that the nephew who helped him gather grain is the Messiah. I can hear him laughing now. How will anyone ever believe my incredible story?

I've told Jesus most of the particulars of his birth, and he seems to understand. I haven't tried to tell any of his brothers, because I'm not sure they will believe me. As much as they love Jesus, it is still unbelievable to think that he is the son of God. They know he is my child. I hope there will be plenty of time to explain his miraculous birth and the promise before they are faced with the reality of the situation. When that happens, James will probably recall the incident with his hand and Jesus' leg. Maybe I should let them read my writings except for the part about Joseph wanting to divorce me privately. They may not believe everything I have written, but at least they will have an idea how the birth happened. Maybe it will help them understand when he must leave to claim his kingdom.

Dear God, please give me the wisdom and the right words to tell Jesus all he needs to know about his extraordinary beginning. Help me to know when the time is right to tell the rest of the children the things they need to be told. Help our other children understand when they realize who Jesus really is. Please give Joseph the strength and good health he needs to continue doing the work he loves. Thank You for blessing me with another wonderfully healthy baby boy.

Jesus Saves his Brothers

According to Joseph, this has been another miraculous day. Joseph's story left no doubt in my mind that a miracle truly happened. The incident caused Joseph much distress. I had to tell him how Jesus had healed James' hand that day he fell out of the tree. He needed to know that we are witnessing small miracles from our son.

Today at work Joseph and the boys loaded a cart of supplies to take to one of their worksites. Filling the cart with lumber and bricks and stones, Joseph tied it down as he usually does. The younger boys were following along beside the cart kicking stones and watching the path. Jesus walked behind the cart to ensure the load didn't shift as it bounced along. While they were moving along, one of the ropes broke and the entire load started to roll off the cart on top of the younger boys. Jesus quickly reached up, pushed the load back and some how reconnected the rope.

Excitement poured from Joseph's voice as he told the story. He couldn't believe Jesus had the ability to hold that big load and mend the rope in one instant without being harmed. I asked him if a bird flew nearby. Looking curiously at me, he related how a bird circled them for awhile and then landed on Jesus' shoulder. Joseph said the younger boys who didn't know the incident even happened were laughing at Jesus talking to a bird. I could only smile as I listened and thought about all the other incidents when the bird miraculously appeared from the heavens. We may have to get used to these happenings. I know we must keep them secret until God lets us know when it is time to make them public. James knows that something strange is happening, but the other children are too young to know that these are really miraculous events.

We were discussing the incident when someone from the village came running up to see if we had seen the doctor. There had been an accident at the sandal shop and the owner, Silas, needed immediate attention. Leaving James and Elizabeth in charge of the children, Joseph, Jesus and I ran to the shop as quickly as possible. By the time we arrived on the scene, the doctor had also. He had already wrapped a cloth around Silas' eyes and was standing there shaking his head. There was nothing he could do now except wait and see how much damage had been inflicted. Silas had been trying to pull apart a cutting tool that was stuck together. As he pulled on the handles with all his might, the cutting part flew open and punctured each of his eyes.

We left after promising Silas' wife that Simon would be down to help at the shop tomorrow. Jesus became distressed on the way home. The incident had greatly agitated him. I could tell he wanted to help Silas, but he knew he could not. He wanted to touch Silas' eyes, but fought within himself to keep his distance. What would his touch have brought? Could a simple touch of his hand heal the man's eyes? Some day God will answer that one for me.

Dear God, thank You for these small but life-saving miracles. I am thankful that You are allowing Jesus to help us with this house full of children even though it is not time for the rest of the world to know of his talents. When I think about all the miracles You have allowed Jesus to perform, I am amazed. I am writing tonight because of the happiness You have given me instead of the sorrow over what could have happened. Help us to remember who he is when we need to know, and to forget when it doesn't matter.

"Aren't all his sisters with us?"
Matthew 13:56

Sarah is Born

Dust again flew from my parchment when I retrieved it from under my cot after over a year. I hope God is not disappointed in the few entries I have written. He would definitely want me to record this event. As I write, my mind is totally astounded at how God can take the most horrible incident and turn it around for His glory. I must write about this most remarkable event before it escapes my mind. No one will ever know unless my recordings are read. Joseph and I decided that we would not have anymore children after Judas; but, as usual, we were a little careless experiencing the wonderful union God made for us. Yesterday I gave birth to Sarah, my third darling baby girl.

This has indeed been my most difficult time. I don't know if it is all the other children and the work that is required or if my body is saying this is enough. God has blessed me with eight children in eighteen years, but after the miraculous happening with this one, I am sure it is enough.

Elizabeth stayed in the room with me and the midwife until my time for delivery. Since she is only thirteen, I did not want her to experience my pain. I do want some grandchildren. The midwife asked her to leave shortly before the severe pains began. When the baby was finally delivered, I heard no cry. The room echoed with the silence of anticipation. I could have heard a feather drop, but no cry could be heard. The midwife tried to revive the baby, but nothing happened. I cried as the baby turned blue. The midwife wrapped her in swaddling clothes and laid her in my limp arms. The strength to cuddle her did not surface. I vaguely remember Jesus walking through the doorway.

"Please leave," he said. "I must talk to my mother." Without question, the midwife slipped out of the room. She was willing to let Jesus say a few last words. As he came closer to my bed, a glow appeared around his outline like the one from the angel who foretold of Jesus' birth. For a moment, I thought I had died and an angel had come to take me home.

"Mother," he calmly said. "Let my Father have control." He took my hand and bent down and kissed my forehead. A surge of energy immediately rushed through my body. My eyes opened wide and my body became whole again.

Then Jesus bent over Sarah whose tiny body had already turned a deep blue. Tears filled my eyes at the thought of him kissing her goodbye. Instead he blew into her dark blue lips. She cried! Her lungs burst forth with the most awesome sound I have ever heard. I cried as a tear slid down Jesus' smiling face. "You must tell no one," he bent down and whispered in my ear as everyone rushed back into the room to see the crying baby.

"What happened?" the midwife wanted to know. "That baby died before I left this room. Mary, you were on the edge of that eternal darkness yourself. How did this happen? What did Jesus do?"

"She only wanted to see her big brother," Jesus said with a faint smile as he left the room and walked outside. The door stood open long enough for me to see the little bird come and perch on his shoulder.

Immediately the room became abuzz with excitement as the women eagerly finished the job they had started a few minutes ago. Someone took Sarah, cleaned her up and wrapped her in some clean swaddling clothes before laying her back in my arms. This time I cuddled her as tightly as possible without crushing her. My urge to run around the room singing praises to God, slowly passed as I thought it would be best for me to act like I had recently given birth.

Finally the room cleared out for me to get some well deserved rest. I didn't need rest. I needed to see Jesus. As if he read my mind, he slipped beside my bed. "Thank you," I said and grabbed his hand.

He only smiled. A gentle smile I knew I would see many times during his lifetime. As he left, I thought how special he really is. He is getting ready for his future and seems to have a good idea of what he can and cannot do. His Father is preparing him for his kingdom.

Lifting my new little girl closely to my chest, we both settled down for some well deserved quite time. I know this must definitely be my last child. There is no way I could dare go through all this again.

Dear God, thank You again for Jesus and his special powers. I know that this baby in my arms would not be breathing if it had not been for the miraculous powers You have given Jesus. I am grateful that You are allowing him to use those powers for his earthly family.

Jesus Graduates from the School of the Synagogue

I have not written nearly as much as I intended when I began this journal. Time is still not my friend when it comes to my writing. God surely has guided me in recording the blessed events of Jesus' life that He chose to be important. I look at the few entries I have written and think about all the events that I have not recorded.

Last night Jesus went to Joseph's shop and came back with a piece of smooth wood. With a piece of charcoal from the oven, he began writing on the wood. When he finished, Elizabeth asked him to read his words. Jesus read the most beautiful prayer I have ever heard. I must add it to my journal. He wrote:

> *Our Father which art in heaven,*
> *Hallowed be thy name,*
> *Thy kingdom come,*
> *Thy will be done in earth,*
> *as it is in heaven.*
> *Give us this day our daily bread.*
> *And forgive us our trespasses,*
> *As we forgive those who trespass against us.*
> *And lead us not into temptation,*
> *But deliver us from evil:*
> *For thine is the kingdom, and the power, and the glory for ever.*
> *Amen.*

There were tears in Elizabeth's eyes, as well as mine, when he finished. It is not only the beautiful words that are moving, but the sentiment he conveys as he recites his work. He wrote the prayer to say at his graduation ceremony.

It is hard to believe that Jesus is eighteen. His formal education is complete. We had a small ceremony to celebrate his graduation with our family and friends and some teachers of the synagogue. Instead of a speech, Jesus prayed the beautiful prayer. His words moved our company as much as they had Elizabeth and me the night before. After the prayer, we had a feast and enjoyed the good fellowship. One of the teachers remarked to Joseph that he feared he "had learned more from Jesus' searching questions than he had been able to teach the lad."

Now Jesus will become a full-time carpenter. Joseph's business will indeed benefit from the addition to his shop. I still expect any day for God to come and take His son to begin the kingdom we were promised, but I also dread it more each day. The longer Jesus stays with us, the harder it will be to give him back.

Dear God, although the entries in my journal are few, they cover many years and offer a sampling of Jesus' home life. There is much missing, but there is also much explained. My duties as a mother and wife are the thief of my time. As busy as my life is, I would not trade my position for anything else You could offer. I only pray that I have recorded the events You wanted to make known to the world. As Jesus ends this important time of his life, I know You will have something great planned for him. Give me the strength to accept Your plan.

Elizabeth's Engagement

The name of my journal needs to be "Special Events in Mary's Life," since that is all I have time to write about. My darling daughter, Elizabeth, was betrothed to Amos today. At fourteen, I feel she is much too young until I remember that I, too, was betrothed to Joseph at that age. They grow up much too fast.

Joseph and I accepted the young man's proposal after Elizabeth informed us that Amos was the one she wanted. It reminded me of our betrothal. I knew the minute I saw Joseph that he would be the one I would marry. Thankfully, Mother and Father agreed which made it easy. Although Jesus and James have not shown much interest in girls, they were eager for Elizabeth to marry this young man. He has been their friend ever since he and his family moved here from Egypt many years ago. They have been best friends since Jesus allowed him to win a race when they first moved here. Now they will be brothers-in-law.

Today Jesus could have his pick of any young girl in the town, but he has no idea he is that handsome. He is much too involved in his studies and his work to please any girl. He did show a little interest in a pretty young girl until she started showing interest back. I don't think he will ever marry nor have children. Evidently his kingdom is not meant for a family.

Since Jesus has become an apprentice with Joseph, he works very long days. When he is finished, he comes home and works on memorizing more scriptures. I think he knows the whole scrolls of Isaiah and Jeremiah. Could he have helped write them? With his interpretation skills, it seems he is reading their minds. He must have watched as the prophets wrote. I have difficulty understanding them, but Jesus can tell exactly what each prophecy means.

Everyone is extremely excited about Elizabeth's wedding. Sarah, who will soon turn four, is anxious to help with the planning. She constantly asks Elizabeth for something to do. This is the first major event for our family in a long time. I must make it one of the most beautiful weddings ever. An abundance of food must be prepared. We must have plenty of wine, which is one of the most important items in our wedding ceremonies. Elizabeth's dress and veil must also be made. Oh, my! I hope there is enough time for all this. I will have a busy next few months. Wouldn't it be grand if I became a grandmother in a few years?

Elizabeth's move to her home after their wedding will create a great void in our family. She doesn't know she is going to become a sister again. I have not told anyone of this pregnancy because I am tired of all the raised eyebrows. With Joseph's energy draining every day, we did not plan for this baby, but we will still love this child as equally as we love all the rest. We know our lives are in God' hands and in about four months, I will again give birth. This has been a strange pregnancy because I have not had the first sign of morning sickness. Usually everyone would have known by now that I am with child, but this time I have not shown any symptoms. My monthly times are such that I thought, or hoped, I had passed the time of the child bearing years, but I guess God planned differently.

It will be different without Elizabeth, but I am certain Sarah will be happy to take her place. I am finally getting used to my family size, and now we will be adding two more. Since Amos is also from Nazareth, I don't believe he will be taking Elizabeth far away. We will gain a child and a son-in-law this year.

Thank you, God, for two blessed additions to our family. I will have another child and a wonderful son-in-law. You have overflowed my life with good family. I pray that You will bless the joining of these two young people with as much happiness and as many children as You have mine and Joseph's. I also pray that Your healing arms will wrap around my dear Joseph and relieve him of the pain he sometimes feels.

Ruth's Birth and Death

This morning I write with such sadness. Yesterday I gave birth to another precious baby girl, Ruth, named after the lovely woman from whom the great King David descended. This truly *must* be my last child. Joseph and I agree we do not want to have any more children. Seven is enough. When I think of Elizabeth having John after being beyond child bearing years, I know that if God wants me to have another one, I will obey him. God also used this child to his glory, but in a much different way.

At first, I had an easy and carefree pregnancy with no symptoms, but the last few months have been the roughest ever. Every time I moved, I would get sick. I was confined to my bed for the entire last month which is hard to do with all the other children. I thank God for Elizabeth and Jesus' help. If Elizabeth had not still been living at home, I would have been lost. She even put her wedding plans on hold to help.

Mother could not help since she has lost all her capacity to remember anything. After coming home so distressed after my last visit, Joseph forbade me to go again until after the birth. Since her memory of me is completely gone, she treats me like a stranger. She lies there waiting for her merciful God to call her home. My soul aches to think of her in that condition. One of her sisters is now living with her. She could come live with us, but I don't think my big family would suit her well.

The sorrow of yesterday will long remain as the worst day of my life. Early in the morning, my ninth child, Ruth, decided she wanted to see this world. I tried desperately to deliver her, but nothing happened. My body had given up by the time the midwife arrived. Little Joseph went to acquire her services, but complications developed with another family that prevented her from leaving. When she did finally arrive, she immediately began shouting instructions which Elizabeth followed. I could tell from the midwife's tone that there was a problem. The pain was different from what I had experienced the times before. I remember the midwife whispering to Elizabeth, as I drifted into unconsciousness. When I awoke from a ripping pain, people surrounded my bed. I could see the tears in Elizabeth's eyes and the concern in Jesus'. The midwife and Joseph were discussing something, but Joseph could only shake his head. Words would have brought tears.

Everyone was ordered out of the room as the midwife began her work. Elizabeth, refusing to leave, wiped the midwife's brow to keep the sweat from her eyes. I felt a sharp pain as I again slipped into darkness. A few minutes or hours later (I still don't know), I regained consciousness and could tell by the look on everyone's face that the ordeal had ended. Elizabeth laid the lifeless body in my arms. I screamed for Jesus to come beside me and for everyone else to leave. The room cleared quickly and Jesus and I were alone. I had carried this baby for nearly nine months. Why? If God had chosen to take her away from me, why didn't he do it earlier like he did Deborah?

"Why?" I asked Jesus, searching his eyes for an answer.

Jesus stood silent for a moment as he tearfully examined the future. Tears filled his eyes as he softly replied, "I couldn't. The pain of her future would have far exceeded what you have experienced tonight. My Father would not allow it." With bowed head, he sadly and slowly left the room. I watched as Blackie joined him, but no bird flew to perch on his shoulder.

What did the future hold for my lovely Ruth? I don't know. I only know that God thought it was more than I could endure. God has a reason for taking babies and I know my sweet little Ruth is whole and peaceful right now in my dear Lord's arms. She and her sister Deborah are singing with the angels.

I later asked Elizabeth to tell me about her, but she could only cry and run from the room. Sitting alone now with my memories and my thoughts, I am deeply saddened at my loss, but thankful for a good and caring Father who knows what is best for all of us and chooses to ignore our pleas to save us from a terrible existence.

Dear God, even in my deepest sorrow, I know that You are still in control. I want to be angry at You for not letting Jesus correct the situation as he did with Sarah, but in my heart, I know You still have control over everything and will allow only what You think is best to happen. Thank You for the wonderful children You have generously given me. I also plead with You to ease the pain that now grips Joseph daily.

Death's Dealt Hand

A timely death is a part of God's plan,
A natural wound that time will eventually heal.
But the untimely death of a child
    is devastating
To think it would be dealt twice to one
    is mind and soul breaking.

He promised us strength to endure all things
    and to be dealt only what we could bear.
He promised hope and a future,
    but without our children what is there?

Hope
    of a better place
    where they are resting in his grace,
    and grandmothers care for them.

A future home
    of love and peace
    where today's sorrow receives a full release.

Comfort
    knowing it is all a part of His plan,
    a child, a mother—death deals the same hand.

Strength
    we receive from inner faith
    to help us understand
    the human injustice of death's dealt hand.

Elizabeth's Wedding

I can finally sing praises again to my wonderful God. After Ruth's death, I felt I had reached the end of my limit. My will to live had been buried with Ruth. I spent weeks inside our room with the curtains drawn thinking about my baby girl. Lots of commotion occupied my house, but I didn't care. I wanted to be alone with my grief. Even Sarah could not bring me out of my deep hole of sorrow. One day when Elizabeth came into my room to ask about her wedding dress, I completely lost my temper. I don't remember ever yelling at any of my children in such a manner.

"How can you think of something grand when I am in such sorrow?" I shouted at her.

"Mother," she calmly replied, "why is it that you cannot look around you and see that life must go on. Ruth's death was a blessing from God. I heard Jesus tell you as much. I need my mother at my wedding, not someone who is blind to God's blessings and is content to dwell in the horrible past. You must give Ruth to God and open your eyes to see that you are desperately needed by many others. Please mother, I need your help for my wedding."

The cloud that hung over my head rose to the sky. My eyes opened and we began making plans for a wedding certain to be the highlight of our lives. We designed the most beautiful wedding dress I have ever seen. The food preparation had been completed well in advance and the entire ceremony ran as smoothly as any I have ever witnessed. I threw myself into Elizabeth's wedding preparations as strongly as I had thrown myself into grieving over Ruth.

Sometimes God does allow us to wallow in the mire of our sorrows, but if we can only keep our eyes open, he will always provide a means to escape that darkness that tries to drag us into a living death of self pity. God took Ruth to prevent her from suffering. Through her death I learned to persevere through the hard times and rejoice in the good times God also gives us.

Today my darling Elizabeth and Amos were married. My heart

rejoices that everything went as planned and that it is over. The last few days have been busy making all the final preparations for this ceremony. With the help of the herbs the doctor gave Joseph, he managed to give her away, but it took all his strength. He is resting now and has been for some time. Of course, if Joseph had not been able, Jesus would have. Jesus is like a second father to them.

What a beautiful wedding. We held it outside under a canopy like mine and Joseph's. We had time to make this one a little fancier. The entire neighborhood came. We have watched these two young people grow up together since they were little children. I greatly missed my mother who passed away shortly after Ruth's death. From the poem I wrote, I can tell I knew of her death because she is taking care of her grandchildren, but I cannot remember one detail of her burial ceremony. An abundance of grief does strange things to the mind. During this wedding, I have learned to speak to her spirit, which has gotten me through a lot of difficult times. She is closer through death than through living the last few years of her life.

As usual everyone laughed and fellowshipped way into the night. Elizabeth and Amos have gone to their house now. It is similar to the one Joseph found for us when we first married. Adjusting to married life for her will be effortless. Preparing meals for only the two of them will be easy for her since she often prepared the complete meal for our big family. If anything, she will have a problem cooking for only two. At least she shouldn't burn the first meal like I did the first time. I hope her wedding night is a little more traditional than mine. Tonight they should find a blessing in the union God established for husbands and wives. I will know from the glow on her face the next time I see her.

Dear God, thank You for giving me such wonderful children. As they grow, I realize how truly blessed I have been. May the rest of my children be as happy as I know Elizabeth is tonight. May they each find the soul mate You have made especially for them. Jesus has a soul mate in You, Father. He loves only You and spends his spare time studying You and Your prophets. I hope You are happy with the few entries I have been able to document of Jesus' life. Much has happened, but most of it is not newsworthy. If I should be writing more, please guide me in that direction. Also, dear Lord, please help me understand Joseph's illness.

Mary Learns of Joseph's Disease

Finally, Joseph listened to my pleading or else he grew tired of listening to my pleading. For whatever reason, he consented to let the doctor examine him. When Joseph agreed to take the herbs the doctor left before Elizabeth's wedding, I knew he was in more pain than I imagined. The herbs did help. He could go for days after taking them with no sign of pain. When the herbs were all gone, I asked the doctor to come back and reexamine Joseph. Had I known what he would tell me, I would not have insisted.

The doctor said Joseph has a disease that is destroying his body. The doctor said it could be in his bones, his blood, his nerves or even in his brain. It is difficult to tell with the limited knowledge that exists for this rare disease. The disease will eventually completely disable Joseph. This could happen within six months or could continue for up to two years. The doctor had not known any patients to live beyond that. The herbs he gives Joseph will enable him to live without pain for awhile, but eventually he will not be able to contain the pain. Joseph will undoubtedly suffer at the end.

When the doctor left, I hugged my darling Joseph and sobbed. He took me by my shoulders and held me at arm's length.

"Mary, why are you crying," he asked calmly. "God has blessed me with a wonderful life. Why should we not rejoice that I have been given over forty years of blessed life and a house full of caring children? We have been through some dreadful times. What makes you think we will not get through this also?"

"Joseph, I cannot bear to live without you or to see you suffer," I replied through my sobs.

"My dear, Mary," Joseph said shaking his head, "do you believe our God will desert us? In all of our years has He ever forsaken us? You know He will supply you with the strength you need."

We sat and held each other until the children came in. Joseph explained to them that he is sick, but the doctor gave him some herbs that would control his pain. Jesus looked at me and I knew he knew. I later saw Jesus sitting under the shade tree with the little bird perched on his shoulder and Blackie lying next to him. He again had to talk with his Father.

When Joseph takes his herbs, he has good days. He says the pain is not getting any worse, but I see how often he must take the herbs. I am concerned that he is quickly declining. He insists he is still capable of caring for himself.

Jesus and James do the traveling now. The business is doing well with Jesus as overseer. He sometimes must travel a day's journey for specialty jobs. The boys love to work for Jesus who constantly encourages them. I heard him tell Simon the other day that he had made the most beautiful scrollwork he had ever seen. Simon beamed. He is only working in the shop three days a week since he is still helping Silas in the sandal shop three days. The boys try hard to please Jesus so he will brag on their work. He is a good carpenter and has no problems keeping the business alive.

Jesus also helps considerably with the younger children's schooling. They love to hear him tell stories. Whenever he has a spare moment, he will go out under the olive tree as they all gather round him while he tells them a story of the prophets. They love to hear about Elijah and Abraham. But their favorite of all times is Jonah and the whale. His stories are beautifully detailed. I could sit and listen to him all day myself.

In the midst of this bad news, Elizabeth and Amos arrived with an announcement that they are going to give us a grandchild. Joseph was elated that he will get to see one of his grandchildren. My heart jumped for joy to think that I would finally become a grandmother. It will be fun having a baby in the house again. It is amazing how God sends a new life to fill the void of a lost loved one.

My dear Lord, I know You are going to take Joseph from me. Can You please let Jesus use his powers to take this terrible disease away from Joseph? How will I ever carry on without him? Why must living be so hard and sad at times? As Jesus wrote in his prayer, if it be your will, please release Joseph from the pain.

Jesus Talking to his Father

Mary Becomes a Grandmother

My, My! What an exciting day. My darling Elizabeth gave birth to an adorable little curly headed boy who reminds me so much of Jesus. For Elizabeth's sake, I hope he is as good a baby as Jesus. At the circumcision ceremony, they plan to name him Joseph after her dear father. He will be proud. It is such a blessing that Joseph is here to see his first grandchild. I realized from experiencing this birth with Elizabeth how much my mother missed by not being with me at Jesus' birth. The birth of the first grandchild is a blessed event.

I wrapped the baby in some swaddling clothes and cuddled him like I have done all of mine. His perfect lips on the ruddy round face circled by dark ringlets of hair looked exactly like Jesus.

I took a trip back to that overwhelming night in the cave when I gave birth to Jesus. It could have been such a bad experience, but thanks to God, it turned into a wonderful adventure. The animals practically ignored us. The shepherds frightened me as they rushed in the stable to praise their newborn king. What an amazing night. Although Joseph and I were all alone, we both knew God had made plans for the care of his son. Every event of that night, from the inn being overly crowded to the shepherds praises, fulfilled one of the prophecies.

I sit here and think about all that has happened since then and I can't help but wonder what has really happened? Joseph and I were filled with such high hopes and aspirations for this new king the angel told us about. The visit of the wise men secured the fact that Jesus truly is the king. Now nearly twenty-three years later, we still wait for that great kingdom to appear.

For years I anticipated many things, but nothing has ever happened. Now I'm not even sure what to expect. I have truly been blessed with a wonderful son, although I expected a king. We have experienced only a few extraordinary events. I have a house full of children, a son-in-law and now a wonderful little grandson. I have been blessed far beyond measure, but it has not been like I expected.

I secretly am still waiting for that great and glorious kingdom. What has happened to it? Surely God has not forgotten us. His son is living here in this house with me. I see his special qualities every day. The things he does, the things he knows. They all point to some divine person leading his way. I am glad I could write about the few miracles he has performed for our family, but no one is going to believe what I have written. When I go back and read them, it is even hard for me to believe those miracles really did happen, and I witnessed them.

The only times Jesus really disappointed me was the death of Deborah and Ruth, and, now Joseph's disease. My wish for my daughters to remain on this earth was selfish, but the wish for Joseph is to ease his pain. Jesus knows I want him to heal his father's illness, but he will not. I have lived with Joseph by my side for many years, I fear I will never be able to live alone. Someday I hope I understand why Jesus wouldn't do these things when he did so easily save Sarah at her birth.

Jesus also chose not to use his powers to save Blackie when he died a few months ago. The poor dog became too old to climb the steps to the roof. Jesus had to carry him up every night and down every morning. When Jesus worked in the shop, Blackie lay close by his side. During the day, Jesus would take him water and food and try to make him eat. One morning Jesus came down carrying a lifeless body.

"Mother," he said with tears gathering in his eyes, "tell the boys I will be late getting to the shop. I have something I must do. I don't want the children to grieve over Blackie. He left this earth last night in his sleep. What a blessing. Oh, if we could all be so fortunate."

He carried the body off toward the desert and didn't return until midday. The children gathered around him asking many questions. He told them Blackie was at peace and would never suffer another minute of his life. Later that day, we all walked with Jesus to take a board on which he had carved 'Blackie' to place beside the spot where he had buried his companion of almost fifteen years. We both knew Jesus had the ability to save Blackie, but his future must not have room for a dog.

With all those powers, why is he still here with us? I don't understand why God is taking such a long time to do something that desperately needs to be done. The people, the country need a Messiah. He is twenty-three years old now and definitely capable of being a king. I worried earlier that something would happen before he became old enough to handle it, but I don't worry about that anymore. At this point in his life, he is capable of doing anything. The problem now is that he is a big part of my life, I am not sure I am capable of letting him go. That sword will truly pierce my heart when his Father decides it is time for him to leave.

Dear God, thank You for this new birth that allows us to remember that life goes on. I want to be the grandmother who loves and cherishes each moment of her grandchildren. My desire is to spoil them and send them home knowing they own a special part of my heart. Please give me the strength and wisdom to accept what You have in store for all of us. If You must take Jesus away from me, please allow me to be a part of the kingdom You have prepared for him. Give me the patience to allow Your plan to be completed.

Joseph's Death

Oh, if I could only take this day out of my chest of memories, for today we buried my darling Joseph. He had become frail and sickly from the monster that was raging within. The doctors could do nothing except give him some herbs to ease his pain. He did not have enough energy to eat. The last few weeks he lay in his bed, like a newborn child. I had to attend to his every need as I watched him suffer.

I should not be writing, but it has been almost three years since my last entry and I need something to occupy my mind. Caring for my darling Joseph became more important than my writing. Journal, you are a dear silent friend that I have missed. I will try to stay in touch more.

The night Joseph told the children their last bedtime story, eight year old Sarah sat on the floor beside him. In a few minutes, all the children had gathered around him. Even Jesus and James sat and listened like little children. The heart-warming scene will long remain in my mind.

Joseph had not been well for some time. He had the disease for three years. The doctor said he had never seen anyone live that long. Joseph was determined to prove the doctor wrong, but he eventually had to give up. The last few weeks Joseph suffered terribly. Many days I sat by his side and watched as he grimaced in pain, only to see the tortured expression quickly turn into a smile when any of the children came to sit with him. They had no idea how badly he suffered. Elizabeth came back to spend the last few days with us to be by her father's side as much as possible. Joseph was proud that he was able to hold his first little grandson. I'm afraid he will not hold the one she is currently carrying.

Once when Jesus came to sit with him, my eyes silently pleaded for him to make it better. I knew from the birth of Sarah, he had the power to cure him. I also knew from the death of Deborah and Ruth that he could not interfere with God's plan, which is different from our wishes. I have learned to respect those differences.

When Jesus stopped at Joseph's side, he bent down and kissed him on the forehead. I heard him thank him for taking such good care of him. Joseph had been slipping in and out of consciousness, but he managed a fleeting smile before he relapsed. He knew and so did Jesus and so did I. Joseph wanted to join his two daughters in heaven. Jesus bowed reverently as he turned and left the room. Joseph slipped away for the last time.

My heart felt like it was being torn from my chest as I walked out of the room of Joseph's death to tell the children that their father had gone to be with his two daughters in heaven. Jesus and the older children tore their clothes over their heart and cried in grief. Jesus recited the prayer accepting the judgment of God for taking the life of a loved one.

Not wanting anyone else to touch his body, Elizabeth helped me prepare him for burial. We closed his eyes, thoroughly cleaned his body and wrapped it in a simple, plain linen shroud. The hot, waxy smell of the candles we lit around his body filled the room. We then wrapped my dear Joseph in a shawl-like tallit. While we were preparing his body, Jesus and his brothers were building a coffin for his burial. As our custom requires, they punched holes in the sides to ensure his body would come in contact with the earth. Our family had some time for a full expression of our grief before any guests arrived.

One member of the family remained with Joseph constantly until his burial. Out of respect we did not eat or drink while in his presence. I could not eat anything anyway. Many came to mourn the death of a dear friend and respected carpenter. The children sorrowfully watched as we laid him to rest. Joseph will always be remembered as a wonderful husband, adoring father and a righteous man in the eyes of his God and his community. During the funeral, a little bird flew overhead for most of the ceremony and eventually perched for a brief second on Jesus' shoulder.

After the burial, my sister, Salome, prepared the meal of eggs and bread for our family. For seven more days we will mourn for our dear father and husband by sitting on the floor, not wearing leather shoes, not shaving or cutting our hair and not performing anything for comfort or pleasure. For the next year, Jesus will recite the mourner's kaddish every day. There are other customs of mourning that we will observe during this year. On the day of the anniversary of Joseph's death, our sons will recite the kaddish in the synagogue. Then we will all light a candle in honor of Joseph that will burn for twenty-four hours. Custom requires we mourn for one year, but I surely will mourn for the rest of my life.

Joseph's physical body may be gone from our presence, but the memory of the righteous man who gave his life to raise God's son will remain in my heart forever. For years we both waited for that glorious kingdom the angel Gabriel promised us. Joseph tried with all his heart to be the father God wanted him to be. When all is known, the world will long revere this man known as Joseph.

Joseph's death also brings to mind that Jesus' responsibility to his earthly father has been removed. The care of the father falls on the oldest son until the father's death. Joseph's death removes Jesus from this obligation. He can now do whatever he wishes. I am hoping he wishes to stay home and help care for all his siblings, but I also know he has a calling that he must respond to someday. If he is going to do something great, I think he will begin soon.

Dear God, my heart is filled with hurt and sorrow for the one taken from me. In my grief, I give thanks for the wonderful life we shared. You are so kind to release him from his suffering. I pray my hurt and sorrow will disappear as timely. Please ease the grip of death that clutches the hearts of our children as they grieve for their beloved father. As we adjust to this loss, take our hand and guide us. Thank You for allowing us to have such a wonderful life after such an unusual beginning.

He is Gone

I loved him
    with a special part of my heart.
My soul mate has left my side.
The bonding we shared as one
    has been ripped apart.

I long to touch him.
To see his smile
To hear his gentle voice
    as he reads to his children
His strong voice
    as he disciplines them.

They are grieving too.
I watch them slip into his shop
    and rush out with tear-filled eyes.
His presence looms over his work.

God chose him to be a special father
    One who would love unconditionally
    One who would cherish each moment of today
    with enough understanding for a new tomorrow.

His soul is again alive
    laughing with his daughters.
He is watching over us
    directing our paths
    from a higher view.

Tomorrow I will see him again.
As we sing a new song
    my soul will be renewed
    knowing that my God is in control.

Today I will grieve for
   the tomorrows I will miss
   the yesterdays I long to relive,
   for today he is gone.

Jesus Conducts the Passover Ceremony

This is my first entry since Joseph's death last year. When a heart is grieving for one deeply loved, feelings are difficult to express. The mind becomes numb as the body moves through the daily rituals until it can again rest in the cave of loneliness. The darkness finally departed as necessity forced me to care for my grieving family. The children were heartbroken. It would have been easy to take everyone into that cave of darkness, but God in his wisdom revealed that there are not enough tomorrows to lose even one by grieving over a blessed event. My dear Joseph has been spared more suffering as he joins Deborah and Ruth. The conversation between God and Joseph about their son would be a blessing to behold.

As earthly life moved on, I realized my job here is not finished. I am required to take on a new role as our family prepares to celebrate the Passover feast. Like Mother, I too love the fellowship that follows Passover. Since I have the biggest family and need to stay busy to keep my mind from wandering back to Joseph's last terrible days, I wanted to prepare the Seder. Tomorrow the boys will travel to Jerusalem where they will again stay with Simon and his family. Sarah is disappointed she will not get to visit with Mary and Martha, but I can't bear to go to that beautiful temple without Joseph. We will celebrate in the synagogue with others who are not able to travel. The boys have stayed with Simon and his family since the first time we met through a mutual friend.

Even though the house filled with family and friends, the fellowship we usually share was muffled by the grief we are experiencing. And yet, in the midst of grief, we received some joyful news. Elizabeth and Amos publicly announced the imminent birth of their second child. I love being a grandmother. It is sad that Joseph will not know anymore of his grandchildren.

Cousin John came as usual. He has always been here for the Passover. After Elizabeth and Zechariah passed away, John still came to celebrate with us. Most of his time is spent in the desert studying with the Essenes. John is a good man, but he seems lonely. With no brothers or sisters,

Jesus is probably the closet person he has to a family. I wish he would come and stay with us, but he assures me that he is happy and likes being on his own. His parents would be pleased with the righteous and devout young man he has become. The feast did not appeal to him. He said he doesn't require much food except the bread and honey he eats daily. Since he looks healthy, I guess whatever he is doing is working for him. I know he misses his mother and father, but I also know he has many fond memories of them.

This is the first time we have observed Passover since Joseph's death. The responsibility falls upon the oldest son to conduct the ceremony. The ceremony itself was beautiful and emotional, but Jesus added his own heartfelt emotions. His sincerity touched everyone.

During the ceremony, John and Jesus kept making eye contact like they knew something more. They were especially nervous when they opened the door to call for Elijah. Compared to the rest of the ceremony, this part appeared different. Usually there is a jubilant shout for Elijah to return, but their shout was hardly more than a whisper. They knew he could not come and they could not put their hearts into calling him. How much do they know? Do they know that Jesus' kingdom will replace the call for Elijah? How will the leaders in the synagogue respond when Jesus tells them he has replaced the coming of Elijah? I tremble with fear of this revelation.

Jesus knows of his birth and of the prophecies. After we buried Joseph, I decided it was time to show Jesus my journal. The two of us went to the roof where I watched his face as he read. He reached over and patted my hand when he read about Joseph's disbelief. He smiled through most of the other entries. But I saw a tear in his eyes as he read about the death of all male babies two years old and under. I still fear what some of my entries would prompt if they fell into the hands of the wrong person. Jesus was so pleased that I had chosen to record these events.

What can Jesus and John really do? What can they accomplish from where they are right now? They are both in their mid twenties, but neither of them has experienced anything of great magnitude. I have waited a long, long time to experience the promise from Gabriel. Perhaps God has chosen to let them live their entire lives as they do now. They both seem happy, but I am beginning to sense a feeling of apprehension especially in John. The fact that they have been here this long with nothing miraculous happening is unbelievable.

The life we live is different from any kingdom I had imagined. It is beyond my comprehension to think what the future holds for these two young men. I fear John may be oversaturated with all the knowledge he has gained. Jesus is the calming factor, but lately he too often stares into the future for hours. I find him more and more sitting under the olive tree praying to his heavenly father. The little bird is nearly always with him. Since Joseph's death, Jesus has been training Joseph and Simon to operate the carpentry business. Although Joseph is only eighteen years old, he is capable of assuming more responsibilities. He knows the business, because he has been working with his father since he took his first step. He appears to be more interested in the trade than any of the rest of the boys. Simon is interested, but he spends a lot of time at the sandal maker's house. I think he is fond of his daughter, Leah. James still chooses to hunt or fish nearly every day to supply our food. Judas follows James as much as he will allow, and the rest of the time he is with his friend, Jacob. Sarah is happy in her own little world.

Dear God, help me understand and help me prepare for what You have already put in place. As my family grows in knowledge of Your word, may You guide them along the path You have prepared for them. Throughout my life I have tried to remain Your humble servant to do whatever You asked of me. I pray for guidance for all of us, as the time draws near when Jesus and John will fulfill the destinies You have created for them.

Sarah Meets her Husband-to-be

I don't know where the time goes. When I opened my journal today, I could not believe it has been nearly two years since I last wrote an entry. I do not have children anymore. They have all grown into young adults. Sarah is now twelve, going on eighteen, and Jesus is almost twenty-eight. It is not as compelling to write when everyone works and life goes by smoothly. Today I wanted to write about Sarah's adventure because I feel it will greatly change my life.

Young love is such a sweet sensation. A few weeks ago Sarah came back from the well with a sparkle in her eyes as she told me she had met the boy of her dreams and someday they would marry. He worked for a caravan going from Cana to Shechem that had stopped for some refreshing water at the well. Sarah said his dark curly hair hung loosely over his broad shoulders as his rich brown eyes pierced her soul. He instantly won her heart. She overheard him talking to the caravan master about coming back through here in about two weeks for the return trip home. That happened two weeks ago and today she has spent most of her time sitting at the well, waiting.

Thank goodness he did make it back today. I did not want to live with her if he had not. Joseph, at twenty-one, has chosen to take on the role of her protector. He also went down to the well—to check things out. He came back smiling with a favorable report. It seems the young man's name is Joel and his family is in the carpentry business in Cana. He is the youngest of five boys and had always wanted to travel with the caravans. For his eighteenth birthday, his father granted him permission to travel and work with this caravan to Shechem to bring back some supplies for their carpentry shop. Joseph said they talked quite a while about the carpentry business, but he noticed that every available chance, Joel's glance strayed toward Sarah. Joseph laughed when he said Sarah broke one of the old laws because she surely looked back from behind her face covering.

Joel told Joseph that he had seen her there on the way to Shechem and purposefully repeated the return date within her hearing. Not knowing that Joseph was Sarah's brother, he asked many questions about her. Joseph said Joel told him he couldn't get her soul-piercing eyes out of his mind the entire time they were gone. He wondered if Joseph might tell him where he could find her parents and maybe he could come back and visit them soon. Joseph smirked when he said the young man became apologetic when he discovered Joseph was indeed her brother.

Suddenly Sarah excitedly rushed through the door nearly attacking Joseph to learn everything the young man had said. Joseph teasingly held her at arms length for quite some time. By that time most of the brothers were in the house trying to find out what had happened to Sarah. They were quite relieved to discover she was only in love. I would certainly hate to be any young man who mistreated that young lady.

It seems I, along with five brothers, have a date with the young man from Cana next month about this time. Sarah may explode before this month is over. I have never seen her this excited. Secretly, I hoped this day would never come. Sarah is too young to be having these feelings about young men. I fell in love with Joseph when I was twelve, but I was much more mature than Sarah is now. With Sarah gone, this house, even with five boys, will seem deserted. I can't imagine staying here without Sarah. The girls have always been my allies. We talk freely about everything with no secrets. Elizabeth and Amos are close enough to visit, but they have their own family now. If someone takes Sarah far away, my heart will be broken.

Maybe this is God's way of preparing me for something else. Once Sarah leaves the house, there is nothing to hold me here. All the boys except Jesus and James are showing an interest in the girls. In a few years, they will be married themselves. They can all manage without me. I will be free to do whatever God calls me to do.

We did have some visitors a few weeks ago. When the boys returned from Passover this year, Lazarus, Mary and Martha were with them. What a delightful reunion. Jesus and Lazarus are true companions. They spent hours walking around Nazareth and talking about everything that has happened on these great hills. Sarah entertained Mary and Martha taking them through all the shops in the village. She really thinks she is as mature as they are.

Yes, my dear God, as one door closes in my life another one is opening. I pray that I am ready for this new adventure which I know is all a part of Your divine plan. I have often thought I could feel the presence of the angel Gabriel during these last thirty years guiding me in a certain direction. May You continue to send Your angel to keep us safe and prepare us for whatever You choose. Thank You for the visit with our dear friends. Your humble servant I will strive to always remain.

Simon's Wife Moves into Mary's house

Our house is becoming smaller every day. Last week I again became a mother-in-law. Simon and Leah, the sandal maker's daughter, were married in a simple quite ceremony at her mother and father's house. Neither Simon nor Leah wanted a big wedding, but they were anxious to be together. Since Joseph's death nearly four years ago, Simon worked some at the carpentry shop, but his desire to be a carpenter was overshadowed by his desire to be near the sandal maker's daughter. He nearly lived at their house this last year. Their exchange of vows did not surprise anyone.

Before the wedding, I moved into Sarah's room and Simon and his new wife moved into mine and Joseph's. It is the largest room of the house and the only one that offers any privacy. They could have moved into her parent's house, but it only has one room and they would have absolutely no privacy. We decided this would work better for everyone. Sarah helped me prepare the "wedding bed." As we worked, she constantly talked about Joel. She knows an awful lot about him, to have only seen him a few times.

We only have the two bedrooms, but sleeping has never been a problem. Unless the weather absolutely prohibits, the boys have always taken their mats to the roof to sleep. Jesus and Simon especially will not sleep inside. That may change a bit, now that Simon has a wife. Or, he and his wife may choose to spend time on the roof. One night during a terrible storm, the boys came inside, but couldn't wait for the rain to cease so they could go back and watch the turbulent, but beautiful, sky. They all like watching the night sky, especially after a storm. Jesus has taught each of his brothers and Sarah the constellations and their meanings. I believe he helped place them in the skies. As much as he knows about them, he had to have a part in their creation.

I knew this would happen. If there were ever two people suited for each other, it is Simon and Leah. Simon expressed his desire to marry Leah a few months ago. Her parents are lovely people who have owned the sandal shop in the village for years. Her father is the sandal maker who was blinded by the accident with the cutting tool. The accident left him completely blind in one eye and only partial sight in the other. He is still able to assemble some finely crafted sandals from memory, but Simon has been going down at least three days a week for years to help him with the cutting and, I presume, take care of his daughter. Jesus and I went to talk to her parents since Joseph is no longer with us. As usual, both parties agreed during the negotiations and were satisfied with the arrangement.

Everyone knew we were not going to keep these two apart. We accepted the dowry and they accepted Simon's price. Everyone also accepted the fact that the marriage would happen soon. Although girls are not supposed to have any contact with men before their wedding, we all had the impression there was urgency for this wedding to happen as quickly as possible. I am sure I will soon be a grandmother again. Reminds me of the urgency of mine and Joseph's wedding, but I don't think Simon ever thought about sending Leah away privately. It is still hard to believe that Joseph doubted my story, and then, at times, it is as equally hard to believe that he ever accepted it.

Did Joseph's parents have doubts of my credibility? Could that be why they never chose to be a part of our family? I often wondered why they moved away shortly after we returned from Egypt and never came back to visit. Were they ashamed of Joseph for marrying an adulteress? Did they disown him? My dear Joseph, did you live with that anguish all your life without telling me? I realize you were a private person, but why didn't you talk to me about it? Alpheus and Simon come by often, but I've never heard them mention their parents around Joseph. I have known Leah and her family for years and know she is a wonderful young lady. There is no reason to doubt their story, but she hasn't been gone for three months. Maybe Joseph's parents did have reason to doubt.

Sarah is the typical jealous sister. She does not think anyone is good enough for any of her brothers. She has voiced her dismay at losing the privacy of her room. If she had not met Joel, I think this situation would be much different. As it is, she knows how young girls are when they desire to be with the love of their life. Joel has been by the house a few times to talk to the boys since his and Sarah's first meeting at the well. Each time Sarah manages to need something from the shop while he is visiting. He walked her back to the house one time to carry the table she desperately needed only to return it to the shop the minute young Joel left. As they walked, I could hear them making small talk. The sparkle in her eyes lasted for weeks. I expect a visit from his parents any day now. If possible I would have Sarah remain with me for the rest of my life. When she moves from this house, I'm afraid the sword will again pierce my heart, but it won't be for Jesus this time.

We have adjusted to the new member in the house quite easily. She is such a shy young girl we hardly know she is here. She is the only child of her family because her father's accident happened shortly after she had been born. Unsure of his future, he did not think he could properly care for anymore children. I am afraid this young girl is going to have a hasty initiation around our busy and sometimes loud family. She is as good a cook as Elizabeth and is willing to do anything we ask of her. Apparently she did most of the cooking as her mother cared for her father's needs.

Elizabeth and Amos announced at the wedding that they were expecting another child in about six months. This will make their third. That is good. The cousins will be close in age like Jesus and John. My family is certainly increasing rapidly.

I saw Jesus seriously looking at Leah's dad's eyes when he came to talk to us. I remember how disturbed Jesus became when the incident first happened. I knew he wanted to heal him, but I also knew he couldn't. His time to be known to the public has not yet arrived and he patiently waits. I wish I knew more of what this waiting will bring. One minute I am anxious and the next I am afraid. What is to happen and when? These questions have haunted me for almost thirty years now. I secretly wish it would all go away and we could live the rest of our lives in peace enjoying each others company.

Dear God, I don't want a kingdom. I don't want a mansion. I want the family and house I have right now. Please make all this unrest go away and allow us to enjoy the serenity we now have. As always, Your bondservant I remain.

Mary's Blessing from God

I am blessed far beyond measure.
God has filled my life with love
    and good children—many of them.
He continually watches over them
    and keeps them from harm.

I still see a little boy taking his first step.
I see a young child running to catch up.
I see a young man standing tall
    as he conducts the Passover feast
    as he works in his father's shop
    as he soothes all his siblings
      at the death of a loved one
    as he becomes the peacemaker
      over two zealous young boys.

My firstborn has grown into a devout man of God.
So I ask You "Oh, God, where is my king?
When will the transformation take place?"

Nothing I have seen resembles a king.
I have heard no chariots or horses
    only the laughter of a house filled with children.
I have smelled no expensive fragrance
    only the dust from bare floors of simple people.

I have thought only of nurturing Your son and my child
    with love and understanding
    and much patience.

I have waited patiently
I have prayed incessantly
I have watched intently
And I have loved unconditionally.

I long to heed Your every desire.
Take me where You want me to go.
I sense Your presence often,
    ensuring that all is well.

I long for the promise You gave.
The son You allowed me to love is going away.
I feel his mission is at hand.

A journey I will not share
    for my sake he will not let me.
I will only watch as a bystander
    and record what must be remembered.

I fear a kingdom is looming
    where the sword will again pierce my heart
    and my son will gain his kingdom and his crown.

The word of God came to John son of Zechariah in the desert
Luke 3:2; John 1:6

John Tells Jesus of his Visit by Gabriel

Cousin John came by for his first visit since the last Passover celebration he attended. He hasn't been here the last few years as he has celebrated with his group of friends. I have asked him repeatedly to come live with us, but he insists he is able to care for himself. I must respect that. His clothes were made of camel's hair and he had a leather belt around his waist. I begged him to stay and eat with us, but he said the locusts and wild honey were his food. He may be teasing me, but I didn't question him.

When John came today to talk to Jesus, he was definitely distraught over something. They went outside and sat under the olive tree for a long time. Jesus sat and listened while John kept jumping up and pacing. He constantly waved his arms and pointed toward heaven. At one time, I overheard him mention "Gabriel." I believe he has been visited by the angel Gabriel, and I know how unnerving that can be. Fear grips my soul as I think what may be happening. Elizabeth always thought John would fulfill the prophecy of Isaiah about the one who would come to pave the way for the Messiah. She was totally convinced that Jesus is Messiah. I know I should be too because that is what the angel said, but I can't imagine Jesus being our great Messiah.

My heart is absolutely ripping apart. I can still remember the words of the angel when he visited me, "the Lord God will give him the throne of his father David, and he will reign over the house of Jacob forever; his kingdom will never end."

I have anxiously waited for that day. For nearly thirty years, I have expected it to happen any time. Sometimes I forgot about it, but then something always happened to again remind me of my extraordinary child. Since Joseph's death, I have had this sensation that Jesus is on the verge of some miraculous happening. For the first time, I fear tomorrow and what it may bring.

From the doorway, I watched John leave. He and Jesus embraced as if they would never see each other again. In my heart, I have the oddest feeling they will never meet as cousins again, but as strangers in a different world. They both smiled as John walked away and Jesus fell to his knees. I thought he might be crying but he praised God and thanked him for John, and his commitment to his destiny. Then I saw the tiny bird swoop down and again perch on Jesus' shoulder. Relief filled my heart as I realized that God is completely in charge.

Dear God, give me the wisdom I need to know what I must do. Although he is Yours, he is also mine. Please don't forget that I have had him for thirty years. To give him up will cause me much pain. Help me to accept and do what You are requiring of me. Your humble servant I will strive to remain.

Mary Reflects on all her Children

I don't often have more than a few minutes by myself. I want to use this time wisely. Simon and Leah have gone to stay with her parents for a few days to help her father with his business. All the other boys have gone on a night time fishing trip with some of their cousins and friends. Sarah is asleep in her bed dreaming sweet dreams of Joel. As I am about to become a grandmother two more times, my desire is to reflect on the status of my children at this point in their lives. While I have the time, it is important to write this because I sense things are getting ready to change dramatically.

It is with pride that I can write something good about each of my children. In a world where children constantly rebel against their parents, God has truly blessed me. I have watched as neighbor's children have been taken to jail for hideous crimes. What happens to some young men that make them so disrespectful and brainless when they grow up? God has indeed given me a house full of righteous, honest, and caring children.

Jesus is my peacemaker and protector. If any of the children are fighting among themselves or with any of the neighborhood children, Jesus is the one who steps in and makes them apologize. If anyone gets hurt he is the first one on the scene. Everything is usually "fixed" before I ever get a chance to see it. He has some miraculous God-given gifts for healing. All the girls faint over his handsome appearance. I know Elizabeth and Sarah have always had lots of friends because they all wanted to come and see Jesus. He has not shown any interest whatsoever.

His love is his scriptures, his Psalms and his Father. I don't know if he talks to him. I've never heard him, but I do know that he will go for long walks and be gone all day. When he comes back he is quiet and reserved. He prays a lot when he is by himself. At his age most men have a wife and family, but he has never shown the first sign of wanting to leave this family. His siblings adore him playing the father role since Joseph is gone. I am thankful, but concerned for him.

My wish is that of any mother—for her children to be happy. If Jesus could be any happier, I don't think he could stand it. I can sense his life is getting ready to take a drastic change. Instead of the joy I once had when thinking about his kingdom, I now have fear. After thirty years, I have this feeling his heavenly father is now ready for that kingdom to begin. When I am near him, I know he is changing. His attitude, his presence, his body are going through a transformation that I can't describe. I can only fear it and pray that I can accept it. Every time I have seen Jesus perform his miracles or read in the synagogue, Simeon's sword gently pierces my heart. Lately I have felt his prophecy has barely touched the surface of my pain. I eagerly but cautiously await my Lord's guidance for Jesus.

James is my provider. He spends a lot of time hunting and fishing to ensure we have food on our table. If there is a different way to do things, James is going to find it. He is constantly performing experiments. I am surprised he has not already left home to be with the "thinkers." He likes to express his views on how things should be done. Unlike the "thinkers," he also wants to get the job done—whatever it is. He searches for things that will test his faith.

He enjoys the company of the party goers and the rebellious boys. Since he comes home every night, I don't think he partakes of their activities, but he does enjoy their company. I know he is a fine, dependable young man. I have no reason to question his behavior. He loves all his siblings from a distance. If they are outside, he is inside talking to me. When they all come in, he goes out. He and Jesus are close, but he only tolerates the rest of his siblings. Sometimes he will do what Elizabeth asks, but it is with reluctance and dread. I think he counts those things as tests to his faith as much as joining the party goers.

Elizabeth is my beauty queen. Her heart has always been in her dancing and her singing. If she could join Pharaoh's dancing girls without participating in the lifestyle, she would be in his palace. I have encouraged her to dance, but her brothers have tried to stop her. They see the dancing girls and the lifestyle they live and know that Elizabeth could never be a part of that. I used to love to watch her sway around the house with her arms spread out and her clothes flying after her. She is light and agile on her feet, or her toes which she walked on a lot. My toes would hurt watching her. I would grimace as she laughed while swaying through the house. If we had lived a different life, her dancing skills would be in great demand.

She became a good seamstress to make the beautiful clothes that we could never afford to buy her. Now she is content to spend time with her husband and two boys, with another child on the way. It is time for her to have a girl. I am glad she married a hometown boy that we knew would be good to her. All the other children adore their brother-in-law and nephews. Thankfully, she and Amos live close enough to visit often which is good for all of us. It is heart warming to have young children in the house.

Then there is Joseph. I never know he is around. Being the quietest of the bunch, he never speaks unless he is spoken to. I used to think there might be something wrong with his voice, but he only chooses to remain silent. He didn't talk at all until he was four years old and then he scolded James for taking something away from Elizabeth. We all jumped and celebrated when he spoke. That embarrassed him so much he didn't speak again for a year, but at least we knew he could. Like Jesus he loves his studies, but he is especially fond of mathematics. Even before Joseph's death, he took care of the calculations for most of their jobs. One of the teachers has asked him to attend an advanced math class for the gifted men. This is one of those classes where they try to solve the earth's problems using mathematics. He is tempted, but I think he fears he may have to speak in the class.

Like his father, his love is crafting masterpieces in the carpentry shop. With experience, his skills will rival his father's. Joseph has primarily taken over the working business of the shop. With Joseph's death, Jesus lost interest in the shop. Luckily Joseph wanted to be more involved. Most of the time, Joseph is in the shop working on a new design for a customer. Using his mathematical abilities, he has come up with some clever creations. I've noticed he stays in the shop unless the young girl down the road comes by to play with Sarah. Then he will choose to come in to discuss his business with me. He watches her the way my Joseph used to watch me. He is only a short step from a wedding. He probably will not want anyone there except his family, if we even get an invitation. I am glad we waited to name him after his father because he reminds me so much of my darling Joseph.

Simon is the next and also the first son to marry. Simon and Leah will be the ones who will take over the household should I not be here. I've noticed that whatever Leah is doing, Simon offers to help. He has watched her do all the work at their house for so long, he tries to make it easier for her. By the gentle way they touch each other, I know they are as much in love as Joseph and I were.

Simeon has become the leader of the customer side of the carpentry shop. He and Joseph have a good relationship concerning the business. Simon deals with the customers and Joseph does the work. As unfair as it may seem, it works for them. Simon doesn't have much time to spend working in the shop since he has taken on the responsibility of his father-in-law's sandal shop. And, I am delighted to add, he will soon take on a new role of father.

Judas, Judas, Judas! What else can I say? At seventeen, he has had more problems than all the rest of his siblings put together. No matter whom he is with or what happens, he is the one that always gets in trouble. A leader and not a follower, he will try anything that has not already been tried. He is not a bad young man nor is he a quiet reserved young man. If he is not first in anything he attempts, he is not happy. His desire is to be as wealthy as the kings, and will do whatever it takes to get there. I pray a lot for him. Every time he leaves the house, I utter a simple prayer for God to please bring him back safely.

With Judas, it is easy to see the influence Joseph had on the boys. Having Joseph around during the important years of the other boy's childhood played a major role in their development. Joseph's death occurred shortly before Judas reached the teenage years, which is a critical point in any young man's life. Even though Jesus took his father's place, I'm afraid we allowed Judas more freedom than Joseph did with the other boys. That freedom has gotten him in trouble a few times.

Although Judas is still sowing his wild oats, he has found a young girl whom I think will soon settle him down. He tells me they are in love. I have never met the girl, but I know her parents are respectable people. A meeting with them will probably be arranged in the near future.

Sarah is my baby doll. As my last child she will always be my precious little baby. Because of the scare at her birth, I consider her my miracle child. And she is. Her servant's heart is apparent in everything she does. When Elizabeth brings her boys for a visit, Sarah sits and rocks and sings beautiful lullabies to the baby the entire time they are here. Thankfully, she did not inherit her singing ability from me.

The heavens and the constellations fascinate her. Thanks to Jesus, she has learned every one of them by name and even makes up some of her own. Jesus has no problem identifying them. They would be easy to remember if you were their creator. Jesus and I see the ones Sarah creates, but none of the others do. At night they often go to the rooftop to gaze at the heavens. Before long all of her brothers will join them. The day she met Joel, the stars told her there would be a change in her life.

Her delightful outlook on life is contagious. When she walks in a room, everyone's spirits are lifted. Sarah adores her older sister and loves spending time with her family. Although Elizabeth is much older, she still makes time to listen and help Sarah with all of her problems. They have always had to share a room at home so they know everything about each other. I have noticed how gentle Sarah is with things. I fear the young man at the well will soon take her away from Nazareth. No matter where she goes she will always be my precious little baby girl—my miracle child.

Then there are Deborah and Ruth. I know they are in heaven, singing praises to God and watching over us. The picture in my mind is Joseph, healthy and strong, telling them a bedtime story. If they had lived, what would they be doing? Would they be as pretty as the other girls? These are questions that will never have an answer, but I know I will see them someday and that is all I need.

God chose to take them away before I ever knew them, but I still miss them and wish I could be holding them right now. They were here for that short period of time for a reason. It would have been easy for Jesus to breathe life into them, but he knew he could not. His maturity had taken over by then and he knew what he had to do. As hard as it was for us, we both understood that he could not interfere with God's plan.

This story is my family. I am missing Joseph now because he did not get to experience all of this with me. Such a wonderful man and Father to all his children, he will never be forgotten. They still often speak of him when they are telling stories or we are eating at the table. Someone will tell a story they remember and we all laugh. Sometimes the laughter brings tears, but they are tears of joy for the memories we will always know. A sincere love for their heavenly father and their earthly family is shared among all of them.

Dear God, I praise You for the wonderful family You have chosen to bestow upon me. Who would have thought when You visited me those many years ago through Gabriel that all this would have happened? Of course, You knew. Joseph and I have delighted in giving Jesus as normal a life as we knew how. I pray that You are satisfied with our life and our family. It is the best that I could offer. Please show me the way of things to come. My responsibilities as a mother will be over soon. The children will be getting married and leaving the house except for Jesus. Only You know what will happen to him. I pray that I will be able to follow him in his journey and continue to record my version of his life. The fulfillment of Your promise is my desire. I fear it is near and I must prepare my family for what is to be. Please give me the strength and wisdom I need. As always, I remain Your bondservant to do Your will.

Author's Note January 3, 2010

"This is my body, which is for you;" I Corinthians 11:24

My book is finished. My modifications are waiting to be sent to Team Tigris of AuthorHouse. My three year project has come to an end. All that is missing is a suitable front cover. I have searched through many paintings of Jesus looking for that perfect image. I trust God will provide my need just like He has so many other things regarding this book. As usual, I am praying for patience.

This morning at Sebring Christian Church in Florida, during the communion meditation by Tod Schwingal, I realized how much this project has touched my faith.

Tod read the familiar scripture of I Corinthians 11:24 about the bread representing the broken body of Christ. I looked at Jean's homemade wafer in my hand as tears filled my eyes. I didn't visualize the broken body of a grown man on the cross as I often do. Instead, I saw the little toddler standing beside his mother in a field of flowers. The broken body on the cross wasn't only the grown man; it was also the newborn baby, the young son of an adoring mother. I felt Mary's pain.

The thought of nurturing a young baby only to watch him abused and sacrificed by some very cruel misguided men overwhelmed me. Even though Mary knew the sacrifice was God's plan, she still felt the pain of losing the son she had adored and embraced for thirty-three years.

My prayer is for all the readers of this book to love that same little boy Mary did. Every time you take communion, feel the sacrifice of a firstborn, beloved son. Feel the pain and weep, but also rejoice that God allowed the suffering because He loves *you* that much.